DOCTOR WHO
THE CURSE OF FENRIC

DOCTOR WHO
THE CURSE OF FENRIC

based on the BBC television series by Ian Briggs by arrangement with BBC Books, a division of BBC Enterprises Ltd

Number 151 in the
Target Doctor Who Library

A Target Book
Published in 1990
By the Paperback Division of
W H Allen & Co plc
338 Ladbroke Grove, London W10 5AH

The BBC producer of *The Curse of Fenric* was John Nathan-Turner
The director was Nicholas Mallett
The role of the Doctor was played by Sylvester McCoy

Printed and bound in Great Britain by
Cox & Wyman Ltd, Reading, Berks.

ISBN 0 426 20348 8

THE JOURNEY OF THE FLASK

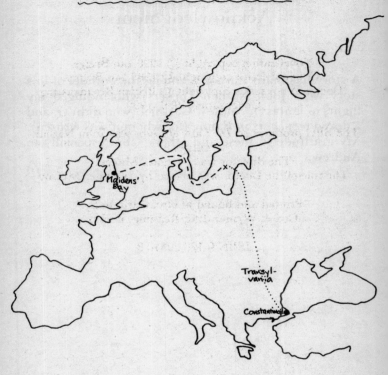

Maidens' Bay

Transyl-
vania

Constantinople

...... Oslaf's journey from Constantinople
---- Hemming's flight to Maidens' Bay
x location where Hemming attacked Oslaf

Acknowledgment

A story has many authors. Among the authors of this story were John Nathan-Turner (who indulged my flights of fantasy), Andrew Cartmel (who didn't), and a dozen teenagers in Ealing (for whom it was written). My gratitude to these and others – but especially to Andrew.

IB

Contents

Dusk

Every story must have a beginning, a middle and an end.

But it's never that simple. Think of the planet Earth, spinning gently round its sun. Someone standing on one side of the planet sees the sun rise on a new day – like the beginning of a new story. But on the other side of the planet, the sun is disappearing beneath the horizon. For someone standing there, it's the end of a story. Sunset in one place is sunrise somewhere else. And for someone who is standing between them, it's the middle of the day (or the middle of the night). It all depends where you're looking from.

All the time, the Earth slowly turns, joining all the stories together – day after day, year upon year. They are joined into one long story with no beginning and no end.

However far back you go, you can never find a first beginning. There's always something earlier.

Does this really matter?

Of course it matters. How do you expect me to tell this story if I don't know where it begins or ends? I could start with a woman standing alone on a beach, but is that really the beginning? Who is she? What brought her here? We might reach the middle of the story and then find that something important took place ten years earlier – or even a thousand years earlier. We'd be in a fine mess then, I can tell you.

Yes, I know, I'm just a grumpy old man and you want me to shut up and get on with the story. You don't mind *where* it begins, just as long as it begins *somewhere*, and I stop talking all this nonsense. All right, then – we'll begin with a woman standing alone on a beach.

But don't say I didn't warn you.

Chronicle I

Betrayal

1

NORTH YORKSHIRE COAST, 1943. She shivered as the cold fog rolled off the sea and enveloped her. Nobody from the village would be able to see her now, which was what she wanted. But she didn't like the fog. It seemed alive somehow, as though it *knew* what it was doing. It was cold, evil and drifted across her skin like the touch of a dead man. She shivered.

She picked up the signal lantern from the sand, and struck a match. The match flame sputtered in the damp air. She pressed it to the wick of the lantern, and a feeble yellow light grew in the gloom. But it threw out no warmth.

She quickly replaced the lantern's shutters, so that no-one would see the light from behind her – no-one would see her treachery – and she turned to face the grey sea fog.

Out at sea – shrouded by the fog, and invisible to the woman waiting on the English shore – the huge, dark shadow of a submarine towered like a sea monster over three small dinghies. Only the red star and some lettering stencilled in Russian on its side betrayed its origin. As the dinghies paddled away and disappeared into the mist, the huge vessel heaved slightly in the waters and began to slip down into the dark depths.

Captain Sorin of the Red Army's Special Missions Brigade had no time to think about sea monsters or evil fog as he drove his paddle through the waves. He barely even noticed the spray of salt water that drenched his face. His only concern now was the success of the mission, *Operation Sea-Wolf*. Sorin had chosen the men himself. He had been allowed to select the very best of the finest commandos in the brigade. They were not only strong and powerful – which he could now see, as they plunged their paddles into the waves and powered the dinghies forward. They were not only completely fearless – experienced fighters who had stared death in the eye and laughed. These men were more than that: they were like machines. No, they were even more than machines. During weeks of training on the coast of the Baltic Sea, they had stretched their powerful bodies to the limit – and then even further. Sorin had driven them to the point where even machines would have cracked and broken, and the men in these three dinghies had looked back at him with unbending loyalty and determination.

But now was the true test.

Sorin's concentration was broken by a shout from his sergeant behind him. 'The third dinghy! It's gone!'

Sorin twisted round to look. To his right, the second dinghy of commandos was still visible, fighting through the water. But to the left, there was nothing but swirling grey fog. The third dinghy was nowhere.

'Keep going!' shouted Sorin. The muscular Soviet

commandos drove the dinghy forward again. 'And keep in sight!'

The sea wasn't rough – they had trained in storms – so how could the third dinghy have disappeared so suddenly? The men in the missing dinghy had been trained to know this part of the English coast in perfect detail. They knew every cliff and cove better than if they'd lived here all their lives. Sorin clung to the hope that they would reach the shore safely by themselves. But how could they have simply disappeared?

For more than an hour the two dinghies plunged through the waves and towards the English coast. The commandos' muscles began to twist with cramp and the men's lungs burned, but the soldiers felt no pain. Pain was just a feeling, and they had been trained to ignore feelings.

'There!' hissed Sorin's sergeant from behind, but Sorin had already seen the feeble yellow glow ahead of them. They headed towards the signal lantern, and the two dinghies crashed over the rocks at the same moment.

The first two men in each dinghy jumped out with their rifles ready – 7.62mm Tokarev gas-operated semi-automatics – and they dropped down to crouch in covering positions. The others leapt into the shallow waters, and grabbed rope handles on the sides of the dinghies. They had practised this manoeuvre dozens of times while training in the Baltic, and with perfect timing they lifted the dinghies and ran towards the cliffs. None of them had ever been within a hundred miles of Britain before, but without even looking they knew exactly where the cave was. They had seen photographs of it taken from every direction, and had rehearsed these moments down to the split-second.

The signal lantern was standing alone on a rock. There was no one about. This too had been planned. *Our agent will leave a lantern on a rock 40 yards south-west of the cave, but they will not stay or make contact. It is important that no one knows their identity.* Sorin took the lamp and snuffed it out. He wondered if the agent was out there, hidden in the fog, watching them.

The men with the dinghies were only just visible now, as they reached the foot of the white, chalkstone cliffs. Sorin made a brief gesture to the men crouched in covering positions, and they followed with huge, powerful strides up the beach to the cliffs.

The cave was well hidden, and from the outside looked like no more than a large fissure at the base of the cliff. Already the other men had slipped through the huge crack, hauling the dinghies with them, and Sorin motioned the look-outs to follow into the darkness. He looked down to the shore. There was no sign of the men from the missing third dinghy. They should have been here by now, but there was no time to wait for them. He turned and followed into the cave.

Inside, a narrow passage led forwards, but Sorin found his way blocked by two of the men. 'What's the matter?' he hissed.

'It's Petrossian.'

Sorin saw a third man, Petrossian. From the moment he had first seen Petrossian, two months ago, Sorin had known there was something different about him. It wasn't just the rough Armenian features that made Petrossian stand out among all the familiar Russian faces. There was something else, something in his eyes – something dangerous – that had made Sorin select him for the mission.

14

Sorin could just see Petrossian's eyes now, as the commandos stood in the cold dark. 'What is it?' demanded Sorin. But he already knew the answer. Beneath the Armenian's rough-hewn expression, Sorin could see a flicker in the eyes. It was not fear, more the awareness of something to be feared.

Petrossian's eyes probed searchingly into the shadows. 'Black . . .'

Sorin suddenly understood why he had chosen Petrossian. Petrossian could feel things that other men couldn't. Like a bat can hear sounds beyond the range of human hearing, Petrossian could sense feelings beyond the range of most other humans – a world of silent rustlings, invisible ghosts, and voiceless thoughts.

Sorin understood this, but the men wouldn't; he had to seem firm in front of them. 'Get in!' he ordered, sounding angry, and pushing all three men into the blackness.

Petrossian had caught only the first shiver of a feeling. He had sensed the shadow of a black nightmare that would soon clutch at their hearts, but he hadn't seen the nightmare itself. He didn't know what was lying among the rocks outside, covered in razor-sharp cuts, frozen in terror and only barely alive.

Of the eight men in the third dinghy, only one men still survived. Only he had seen the nightmare.

2

'If this is a top secret naval camp, then I'm Lord Nelson,' complained Ace.

She had been expecting a high-security dockyard, full of secret submarines and torpedoes and things like that. Instead, the Doctor had brought her here. It looked like a dozen huts made out of corrugated iron, and a few old stone buildings.

'Well, the uniforms seem about right,' observed the Doctor, watching a couple of figures that drifted across the open compound. 'British Navy, early 1940s.'

This made Ace's mood even worse, because it reminded her of the stupid clothes she was wearing. Not only did this 1940s clothing look naff, but everything felt all rough and prickly. She would die of shame if any of her mates in Perivale ever found out that she'd once worn a pair of size 18 bloomers.

She hitched the duffle bag over her shoulder in annoyance. 'Professor, top secret naval camps have men with guns all over the place. You don't just stroll in.'

The Doctor looked round. Ace was right. There was something wrong here. The Second World War was at its height and fear of Nazi spies was everywhere, yet nobody had tried to stop them as they strolled through the main gates. Nobody had even appeared to notice them.

But Sergeant Leigh was watching the two strangers through his binoculars from inside the guard post. Still not 20 years old, the marine was hard like stone as he murmured a pre-arranged code into a radio. 'House guests leaving the conservatory. Approaching the library.' His voice had an edge that was flint-sharp.

In the command room, located in a hut at the other end of the camp, Captain Bates leaned forward to listen to Leigh's words. The sergeant's voice cut through on the radio again. 'They'll reach the drawing room in about sixty seconds.'

Bates smiled, as the two strangers walked further and further into the trap.

Ace looked around suspiciously. 'I've had more trouble getting into Greenford disco without a ticket,' she muttered.

The Doctor was getting cross. 'You can always go back.'

'You promised me I could go rock-climbing. Fat chance,' grumbled the teenager. She turned and looked back to check behind them.

Leigh saw her face. He grabbed the radio and hissed angrily, 'Something's wrong! One of them's a girl!'

Bates stiffened in the command room. 'Say again, sergeant.'

The radio crackled. 'One of them's a girl, sir! They're the wrong ones!'

Bates rapidly made a decision and barked orders into the radio. 'Rat-trap! Rat-trap *now*!'

Leigh quickly turned to the three marines who were waiting with him in the guard post. 'Move it!' he shouted.

Instantly, in a flurry of movement, the Doctor and Ace were surrounded by a dozen marines who suddenly appeared from empty doorways and corners. Each man trained a gun on the two companions.

'Don't move! Hands up!' ordered Leigh.

The Doctor turned on Leigh with an angry face. 'About time too! Call this His Majesty's Royal Navy? Disgraceful! We could have been German saboteurs!'

The sergeant was taken by surprise. He snapped to attention – the stranger was clearly an officer of some sort.

17

The Doctor saw that his plan was working nicely, so he continued. He spun round to face another of the marines. 'And those boots are filthy, marine! What would happen if the Germans attacked now? We'd have to write to your mother and tell her you died in filthy boots!'

'Sorry, sir,' mumbled Perkins, the unfortunate marine.

Ace decided to join in the fun. She turned furiously on poor Perkins. 'In fact, how do you know we're not Germans?'

'You don't look like Germans, ma'am,' stammered Perkins.

'Have you ever seen a German?' demanded Ace. 'Complete shambles!'

The Doctor glared at Leigh. 'I'm putting you on report, sergeant. Your men are an utter disgrace!'

'Yes, sir!'

'You probably don't even know which one is Dr Judson's office. Never mind, we'll find our own way.' The Doctor pushed through the marines towards one of the huts. Ace marched behind him.

Dr Judson reached upwards from his wheelchair and scribbled furiously. The blackboard was covered in mathematical equations and logic flow charts, a maze of lines and junctions. His legs were paralyzed and his body was frail and weak, but the intense expression in his face was that of a genius. Nurse Crane knew to keep out of his way when he was in a temper. Any more strain and his heart might fail completely.

The door flew open and the Doctor strode in.

'In heaven's name!' exploded Judson at the interruption.

The Doctor stepped forward, smiling. 'Ah, you

18

must be Dr Judson. Pardon the intrusion. We've travelled a long way to meet you.'

'This is intolerable!'

Nurse Crane tried to calm her patient. 'A little less excitement please, Dr Judson. Remember your blood pressure.' She turned sternly to the two strangers. 'Now, look here. You can't just stroll in like this.'

Ace smiled apologetically. 'That's what I told him.'

But the Doctor wasn't interested in all this. He had noticed one of the diagrams on the blackboard. 'The Prisoner's Dilemma.'

Nurse Crane looked at him. 'If you two don't leave at once, I shall have to . . .'

'Shut up, Crane!' interrupted Judson. He didn't recognize the two strangers, but the oddly dressed little man evidently understood the flow charts. 'You're familiar with the Prisoner's Dilemma, then?' he asked the Doctor.

'Based on a flawed premise don't you find, Dr Judson? Like all zero-sum games. But I must compliment you on the elegance of your algorithm.'

Dr Judson was startled. His work involved the most advanced mathematics in the world. He was recognized as a genius throughout Europe and America. Even the Nazis whispered his name. Yet here was a complete stranger who discussed it like a piece of school homework.

The Doctor glanced up for a moment as though he had just remembered something. He looked round the office. 'Do you have a sheet of official stationery and a typewriter I could use?'

'On the desk,' gestured Dr Judson, bewildered.

'Thank you.' The Doctor retrieved the typewriter from beneath a pile of books and put a sheet of War Office paper in it.

Dr Judson began to recover from his astonishment. 'You're clearly also an expert in this field, but I don't think we've ever . . .'

The Doctor concentrated on his typing and just waved a hand vaguely. 'Ace . . .'

Ace stepped forward to do the introductions. 'Hi, I'm Ace and this is the Professor.'

'Doctor,' came the irritated correction.

'Sorry, the Doctor. I always get it wrong. Wow, have you seen this, Professor?' Ace had just noticed something on the desk. She picked it up. The device was about the size of a book and made out of wood and brass. An array of circular holes on the front showed either blue or yellow inside.

'Put it down, child,' said Judson crossly. 'It's not a toy.'

There was a sharp edge to Judson's voice. Ace quickly put the device down. 'I know it's not a toy,' she apologized. 'It's a flip-flop thingy. We had them at school.'

Judson was amazed. She was just a girl – a mere child. 'You understand it?'

'Yeah, it's a logic game.' She picked it up again. 'Look. You drop these marbles in the holes along the top and depending what colour each window on the front is, the marbles fall down different paths inside. You've got a logic diagram for it on your blackboard.' She pointed to one of the scribbled chalk mazes.

'Extraordinary. And you learned about logic at school, you say?'

'Yeah, Miss Sydenham taught us in computer studies. She was well good. Can I borrow this?'

The girl was clearly a student at a top secret academy, where the most brilliant children were being trained to become the scientists of the future. Even

Nurse Crane – who never seemed to take any interest in Dr Judson's work – was looking curiously at the girl.

'Pens!' announced the Doctor. 'I need two.'

Judson gestured to Crane, who found two fountain pens for the Doctor.

'Thank you.' The Doctor took a pen in each hand and simultaneously scribbled with both at the foot of his typing. He straightened up and fanned the paper to dry the ink. 'Come in,' he called.

Judson and Nurse Crane looked round, wondering who he was calling to. Suddenly, the door burst open. Captain Bates rushed in.

'Sorry to disturb you, sir, but these two are unauthorized personnel.'

The Doctor turned sharply on Bates. 'Unauthorized? We are here at the urgent request of the War Office, captain.' He handed the sheet of paper to Bates, who quickly read it.

To whom it may concern.

The bearer of this document, Dr (there was a splodge of ink over the name), *is to be allowed free access to all areas of the North Yorkshire Signals Camp, and provided with whatever information he requires. These facilities are also to be made available to his assistant, known as code-name 'Ace'.*

(Signed)

'I think you'll find it's signed by both the prime minister and the chief of the secret service,' smiled the Doctor.

'I do apologize, sir. We weren't warned of your arrival.'

'*Need to know*,' explained the Doctor. 'Only people

21

who needed to know were told. Security is vital. Dr Judson's work at breaking the German codes is crucial to the war effort.'

'We thought you were something to do with those East End kids – the evacuees who arrived in the village this morning.'

'Here, I'm not from the East End,' bristled Ace. The Doctor trod gently on her foot as a signal to shut up. Ace wasn't happy, but she kept quiet.

Judson hadn't noticed any of this. He was too concerned to get to know this new colleague better. His eyes blazed as he excitedly turned to the Doctor. 'Perhaps you'd like to see the Ultima machine, Doctor?'

The Doctor's eyes lit up. This was what he had come for! 'Ah yes, the Ultima machine.'

Judson turned to Bates. 'Captain, go and fetch Commander Millington.'

But on hearing the name, the Doctor had second thoughts. 'Commander? Um, no, actually it's been a tiring day. Perhaps we'd better leave it until tomorrow, Dr Judson. If you could just show us to our quarters, Captain.'

It was easy enough to fool a sergeant or a captain with a bit of paper, but the base commander was a different kettle of fish. The Doctor wanted to find out what was going on before he met the base commander.

The gloom of the fog seemed more powerful as the last lingering traces of daylight grew weaker. It would soon be night.

Sergeant Trofimov was on watch. From the cave entrance, he surveyed the beach through binoculars. He knew there was something out there, but he couldn't see what. The tide was going out, and he scanned the water's edge, looking for anything from the missing dinghy that might have been washed up.

Suddenly, he saw something move. His muscles tensed and his breathing grew faster. A younger, less experienced soldier wouldn't have seen anything. But the younger, less experienced soliders didn't live to repeat their mistakes.

Trofimov looked again, out into the falling night. Down on the rocks, he could make out a shape. It looked like a body. He saw it move again. And then he saw the uniform of a Red Army commando. It was a survivor from the missing dinghy.

Trofimov turned back into the cave.

A couple of metres back into the rock, the passage opened into a small cavern. The other commandos were busy deflating the two dinghies, and storing equipment.

'Quick, down on the beach!' Trofimov hissed urgently.

A number of the men automatically grabbed their Tokarev semi-automatics, and looked to Sorin for orders. Sorin nodded for them to follow Trofimov.

They hurried out of the cave after the sergeant. Only Petrossian hung back, scanning the dark of the cave as though listening for something. He glanced at Sorin. 'How long until nightfall?'

'Long enough,' replied Sorin. 'What is it? Can you hear something?'

'I don't know. Voices in my mind.'

'What are they saying?'

'There are too many of them – too many voices. I can't make them out.'

'Don't tell the other men. They won't understand. Come on.'

* * *

23

Trofimov's boots crashed over the rocks as he raced towards the body that lay in the shallow waters. Other commandos dropped into covering positions. Shortly, Sorin joined the sergeant: the two men knelt beside the wounded man.

Sorin recognized him as Corporal Gayev, leader of the commandos from the missing dinghy. Gayev's flesh was cut deep with razor-straight lines, and he was weak with loss of blood. Sorin looked in Gayev's tunic pocket. The package of secret orders for the men in Gayev's dinghy should have been there. But the cuts had slashed the pocket open, and it was empty. Sorin turned Gayev's face towards him.

'Gayev, listen to me. Where are the sealed orders? You had them. What happened to them?'

But he knew from the corporal's face that he wouldn't get an answer. Gayev was still alive and conscious, but the expression in his eyes was frozen. His mind was trapped behind a wall of solid ice.

Petrossian reached out to touch Gayev's face. He sensed the ice, but he also felt the terror behind it – a terror so sharp and penetrating that Petrossian could feel it even through a wall of ice. He looked at Sorin.

Sorin knew what Petrossian wanted to tell him, but this wasn't the time or place. He could also feel the other men looking at him for leadership, so he quickly issued instructions. 'It's getting dark. As soon as it's night, we'll go and check the British camp. Petrossian, you stay and check the shoreline in case anything gets washed up.'

'We ought to work in pairs,' remarked Petrossian.

'We don't have enough men to work in pairs. We're already eight short.'

'We still ought to work in pairs.' Petrossian looked

out into the swirling fog. 'There's something here . . . Can't you feel it cold against your skin?'

Sorin decided to make a joke of it, and take everyone's minds off the missing men.

'More of your Armenian superstitions?' he laughed. The other men smiled, and Sorin went on. 'You're supposed to be a solider!'

Petrossian looked down at Gayev. 'So was he.'

The smiles disappeared, as everyone looked back at the man with the frozen, staring eyes.

'We follow orders,' replied Sorin.

'Ace! Bunk beds! Bags I go on top!'

Ace ran into the small bunk room, and threw her duffle bag onto the top bunk. One of her friends at school used to have a bunk bed, and Ace had always wanted to sleep on top of one. She hauled herself onto the top bunk, and looked round excitedly. The room was pretty empty. It contained just the bed, a cupboard, a chair and a paraffin stove that glowed in one corner, but it felt like being king of the castle!

Ace kicked off her uncomfortable shoes, which landed noisily on the wooden floorboards.

'Quiet, Ace. People are trying to sleep.' The Doctor frowned at her.

'Sorry.'

The Doctor sat on the edge of the lower bunk. His mind, however, was clearly elsewhere.

Ace's head suddenly appeared behind him, hanging upside-down from above. 'Is it all right if I go down to the cliffs tomorrow and do some rock-climbing?'

But the Doctor was in one of his moods. He turned to her in annoyance. 'Go to sleep.'

'Sorry.' Her head disappeared.

25

'Put that light out in there!' shouted a voice from outside.

The Doctor stood up and went to the light switch by the door. He paused for a moment as though he sensed something. Then he switched off the light.

The yellow glow that had warmed the room was replaced by the blue shades of night from outside. Shadows reclaimed the corners that were hidden from the window. A room that a moment before had seemed reassuring and safe, now felt alien and threatening.

'Goodnight,' called Ace, to reassure herself that she wasn't alone. But the Doctor didn't reply. She turned to look at him. He stood by the window, the dark shadows on his face making him look older – older and more powerful. It was a dark, ancient power which he kept hidden by day.

The Doctor turned and moved towards the door.

'Where are you going?' called Ace.

He looked back at the girl. 'The night air. Go to sleep.' In the light from the window, he saw her large, anxious eyes. Then he left her.

Ace lay back in the dark. She could hear faint noises all around her. It was probably just wooden timbers creaking or the wind finding a gap somewhere, she told herself. But why had she only just noticed the noises?

She reached for her duffle bag, and took out the flip-flop game. She dropped one of the marbles through it a couple of times, watching it flip-flop down behind the coloured windows. But she couldn't concentrate to play the game properly, so she stopped. She lay back and stared into the shadows in the roof.

A baby cried.

The noise seemed to be coming from another room

in the hut. Ace listened to the baby. Then she heard its mother's voice, a soft, young northern voice that was full of love and gentleness. 'Shh . . . don't be scared. Mummy's here. Shh . . .'

A lonely tear trickled across Ace's cheek.

The chill of night hung over the naval camp. All lights had been extinguished – as they had been throughout the entire country – so that night-time German bombers would have no way of finding their targets. The camp was dark and silent.

Along the perimeter fence, a naval guard paced slowly. He didn't like night duty. It wasn't the dark he disliked so much as the cold. When you first stepped outside, it never seemed to be all that cold, but the chill soon reached down to your bones. And it was a black, unnatural cold.

He stopped and listened. A steady footfall came from the shadows; whatever it was had a slow, measured pace – and it was getting closer.

The guard's breathing quickened, and his pulse began to race with fear. He quietly slipped his gun from his shoulder and raised the weapon towards the sound. The footsteps grew closer.

His finger tightened on the trigger as he peered into the shadows, trying to make out the stranger. He thought he could just about see the outline of a figure approaching. He raised the gun a little higher and pulled his finger back slightly on the trigger. He could feel a rapid thumping in his chest. The figure began to emerge from the night.

The guard could see his face now.

He sighed with relief to realize that it was the oddly dressed stranger who had arrived with a girl earlier in the evening. 'Oh, it's you, sir. Thank goodness. Gave me a bit of a fright there, I don't mind admitting. I thought . . .'

But the Doctor wasn't listening to him. Instead, the Doctor turned and looked into the darkness beyond the perimeter fence. 'Eyes,' he murmured. 'Eyes watching.'

Sorin's eyes followed a second guard who was patrolling the opposite end of the camp. Sorin was hidden in the woods a short distance from the camp. As the guard passed a ditch that ran between the woods and the camp, Sorin clicked his stopwatch and looked at the time: five minutes and twenty seconds.

This was crazy. All night long, the gap between guards had never been less than four and a half minutes; sometimes it was as much as six minutes. A bunch of schoolgirls using nail-scissors could cut through the fence in less time than that! This was no job for the Red Army's Special Operations Brigade. Half a dozen ballerinas from the Kirov Ballet could have handled the job.

The British were clearly being careful not to draw anyone's attention to the camp with a high security presence. The official Navy explanation for the camp was that it was merely a signals camp: a few women who monitored German radio signals, nothing important. (Certainly nothing as valuable as the Ultima machine.) So the security was clearly intended to give the impression of just a small, unimportant naval base.

Sorin briefly wondered who the British Navy was trying to keep from discovering the secret: German spies or the British Army. He smiled as he thought of the unholy row that would break out if the British army ever found out what its colleagues in the navy were up to. At Bletchley Park in Buckinghamshire, the army had gathered some of the best mathematicians in the country to build a machine that would decipher the German Enigma codes. And here, at a remote camp near the North Yorkshire coast, the navy (which could never quite bring itself to trust the army) had secretly decided to build a rival machine. While Dr Judson, the crippled genius, was forging ahead with his Ultima machine, the Bletchley Park boffins were still struggling to stop their machine from overheating.

Still, Sorin knew that the weak security was only on the outside. He expected heavy fighting once his men were inside the camp, but his men were ready for that. Tomorrow night, the British wouldn't know what had hit them!

In the shadows of the unlit beach, Petrossian's boots crunched softly as he walked along the shore. The fog was all around him and he could see only a few paces ahead. So far, he had found a pistol belonging to one of the missing commandos, but no more bodies. The chambers of the pistol were empty: all the bullets had been fired. The missing dinghy had evidently been attacked. If it had simply overturned in a large wave, there would have been no need to fire any bullets. But who – or what – had attacked the men?

Petrossian noticed a package lying a few metres away. He picked it up, and peered at it in the dark. It was a waterproof envelope with Russian lettering on the cover: *Cpl Gayev – to be opened only in an emergency.* Petrossian broke the seal.

He drew some papers out of the envelope. On top was a large photograph of Dr Judson.

Then he heard the voices.

29

They weren't human voices, and he didn't hear them with his normal hearing. He heard them in his mind. But he knew that they were coming from somewhere close by him.

He looked round, but there was nothing but fog. He sensed that the voices were approaching from behind him. He dropped the package and started to back away. But the voices followed him. Even in the fog, they knew where he was, and they followed him.

The voices grew stronger in his thoughts. There were three or four of them, strange echoes in his mind, and they seemed to be saying – or thinking – the same thing: the fluid of life . . . seek out the fluid of life . . .

Petrossian turned to run, but then he realized that more voices were approaching from ahead of him. He was trapped.

The voices grew closer: seek out the pure fluid . . . the fluid of life . . .

Then he saw them, figures emerging from the fog. And he knew them. They were the missing commandos. But they were changed. Their ghastly white faces were the faces of dead men, and their mouths were swollen. As they approached they lifted their arms towards Petrossian. Their fingernails glittered like steel razors. Terror gripped Petrossian tight around the chest.

The pure fluid of life . . .

'No . . . It's me – Comrade Petrossian. Don't you remember?'

We remember you.

Release us, Petrossian. Give us death.

'I don't understand . . .'

If you can't give us death, then give us life.

The fluid of life . . .

They began to advance on Petrossian once more.

He backed away and turned, but they were all around him, reaching towards him with their razorblade fingers. He felt the fingers slice across his neck. There was no pain, but a warm liquid ran down his neck.

The pure fluid of life . . .

3

The parish church of St Jude's seemed to loom out of the morning mist like a small fortification. It was an unusual building: a squat chalksone tower flanked by two grey slate turrets. If it weren't for the surrounding graveyard it wouldn't have looked like a church at all.

A thin trickle of villagers, all dressed in their grey Sunday best, were making their way home down the country lane. Only Miss Hardaker, a sharp-faced spinster in her fifties, and two teenage girls lingered on the church porch where the young vicar listened patiently. Miss Hardaker was determined to make her point.

'There's no doubt about it, Mr Wainwright. Of course we shall win the war. Right is on our side.'

The two girls fidgeted slightly in boredom.

Mr Wainwright remonstrated politely. 'I'm not sure that right is on anyone's side in war, Miss Hardaker.'

The spinster's beady eyes turned cold. 'Your father must turn in his grave to hear such words. When he was vicar of this parish, there was respect for the Good Book.'

'Surely faith is more than just words.'

'In plain language, doubt and indecision, Mr Wainwright.'

The Doctor strode purposefully down the church path. Ace followed a little way behind him. Miss Hardaker glared at the two strangers, but the Doctor smiled cheerily and raised his hat.

'Good morning. I wonder if you could help us. We're looking for Dr Judson.'

Mr Wainwright turned back into the church with the Doctor following, but Ace had gone to find out who the two girls were. They seemed to be about the same age as her, and from their bored faces she guessed that this wasn't their idea of fun. 'Who's the gargoyle?' she asked, looking back at Miss Hardaker. 'Friend of yours?'

'She's the old bag we've been billeted with,' complained one of the girls, who looked a few months older than the other. She had cool blue eyes, and her blonde hair was tightly wound and pinned up. The other girl has a round, smiling face, and her eyes were a rich chestnut brown.

Ace wasn't sure what the blonde girl was talking about. 'Come again?' she asked.

'Me and Phyllis have been evacuated,' explained the girl. 'The Blitz and all that.'

'We're from London,' added Phyllis.

'Yeah, me too,' grinned Ace. At last, she thought, some normal people!

'Now then, girls. Time we were moving.' Miss Hardaker' sharp voice cut through the thin mist.

The blonde girl groaned. 'Back to the Land of the Dead.'

Ace couldn't let them go without arranging to meet again. 'Can you get away after lunch?'

'We'll sneak out while the old dragon's sharpening her teeth!'

'Where shall we meet you?'

Ace looked back at a signpost that stood in the lane. It read: *Maidens' Point, 2 miles.*

Phyllis laughed. 'Maidens' Point? Well, that rules me and Jean out, for a start.' She had a warm laugh.

'And me,' added Ace, joining in the conspiratorial smiles. 'See you later, girls.'

Jean and Phyllis laughed, and turned to follow Miss Hardaker.

Ace hurried into the church to catch up with the Doctor.

The Doctor and Mr Wainwright were at the far end of the church, heading towards a small door at one side. Mr Wainwright was talking to the Doctor. 'I can't see why he spends so much time on some old carvings. I keep telling him it's pointless.'

'Answering questions is never pointless,' responded the Doctor.

Mr Wainwright turned to look at him. 'That depends on the answer.'

Ace caught up with them as they reached the small door. 'We're not going to be here long, are we, Professor? Only I've arranged to meet Phyllis and Jean later.' But the Doctor wasn't listening: he was thinking about Mr Wainwright's last remark. The two of them followed the young vicar through the low doorway.

They found themselves in the vestry, a small room where the vicar prepared for each service. Two more old wooden doors led out of the room; Dr Judson's empty wheelchair stood by one of them. Ace saw in amazement that a couple of solid silver candlesticks and a solid silver plate were lying on a table.

'Here, vicar. You shouldn't leave all this silverware lying about. You're wide open for getting it nicked.'

'Oh, they're superstitious folk in these parts. Too much afraid of the old Viking curse to break in here.'

Ace's eyes opened wide in surprise. Even the Doctor looked round.

'Curse?'

'The church is built on old Viking graves,' explained Mr Wainwright. 'They say evil was once buried here.' He opened one of the low doors. Behind it there was a spiral stone staircase that led up and down. 'The crypt is down here. If you'd like to follow me.'

The Doctor followed Mr Wainwright down the stairs. Ace hung back for a few moments. Through an old window by the third door, she could see the graveyard outside. She tried shaking the door. The lock on the inside was old and rusty. It wouldn't take more than a decent kick to smash the door open. That silverware wouldn't have lasted more than a week in Perivale. The people around here must be unbelievably honest. Either that, or very frightened.

Ace followed the other two down the unlit steps. It seemed to grow colder as they descended under the church. A little way down, though, the darkness gave way to the faint yellow glow of an oil lamp down in the crypt.

At the bottom, the stairs opened into a low-ceilinged chamber with stone walls. The stones weren't the regular blocks used for building, but huge slabs like enormous gravestones. They were old and worn, and covered in the faint marks and lines of ancient Viking inscriptions.

Sitting in a rickety wooden chair was Dr Judson. Nurse Crane was holding an oil lamp in front of the wall, and Judson was peering at the inscriptions in the dim light and marking copies of them in a notebook. His eyes glittered ravenously. 'Ah, Doctor!' he exclaimed, as he noticed the new arrivals emerging into the oil lamp's glow. 'What do you make of these, then?'

The Doctor inspected the markings. 'Fascinating. Look at these, Ace.'

Ace stood by the Doctor. She vaguely recognized the stones from pictures in school history books. 'They look like Viking carvings.'

'Viking rune stones,' corrected the Doctor. He turned to Dr Judson. 'Ninth century, yes?'

'You evidently know more about it than I do,' retorted Judson. He was a little annoyed to discover that the strange little man was an expert in Viking history as well as mathematics.

'It's the alphabet,' explained the Doctor. 'The later Vikings used a shorter, 16-character alphabet.'

'Don't tell me,' Dr Judson interrupted before the strange little man had a chance completely to spoil his fun. 'I enjoy the challenge. The Ultima machine can break the most sophisticated Nazi ciphers. Some ninth-century scribblings shouldn't be much of a problem!'

Ace stood by the other wall and thought how stupid people were. They thought it was wonderful that Vikings used to scratch dots and lines in stone walls, but complained when teenagers used spraycans to paint colourful graffiti on boring grey concrete. But her thoughts were interrupted by a noise, the kind of hissing sound that could have been made by huge kitchen equipment. She looked round but couldn't tell where it was coming from.

'Here, Professor, what's that noise?'

The Doctor turned to listen, but the noise had stopped. 'What noise?' he asked.

'Like those big hissing things they have in the school kitchens.'

'Probably the organ bellows. Come on, let's leave Dr Judson to his puzzles.'

'Yeah, OK – it's just . . . I could have sworn . . .' But the Doctor had disappeared back up the spiral steps, and Dr Judson had returned to his rune stones.

'No, it was definitely some kind of machinery, Professor.' The Doctor wasn't taking any notice. He was looking round the graveyard outside. Ace trailed after him. 'But don't bother listening to me. I'm only the waitress,' she grumbled.

'Look,' called the Doctor, pointing out some overgrown graves.

'Yeah, graves.'

'No, look at the ground.'

Ace looked. 'Oh yeah, there's a sort of dip in it.'

A slightly sunken channel – maybe a metre or two wide, and twenty or thirty centimetres deep – ran through the graveyard away from the church and towards the woods. The signals camp was on the other side of the woods.

'It's caused by subsidence,' observed the Doctor. 'And it happened after the graves were dug.'

'How do you know that?'

The Doctor went up to one of the graves on the edge of the dip. The gravestone was leaning at a precarious angle. 'Well, either that, or they'd been knocking back the communion wine when they put this headstone up,' he smiled.

Ace read the lettering on the headstone. It was covered in damp green lichen, but she could still make out the words:

Joseph Sundvik
Born 8th April 1809
Died 3rd February 1872

Florence Sundvik
Born 3rd July 1820
Died 12th January 1898

Mary Eliza Millington
Born 4th March 1898
Died 17th March 1898
'Suffer the little children
to come unto me'

'Sundvik,' murmured the Doctor. 'They must have been descendants of the early Viking settlers.'

'Look at the last one. She lived only thirteen days, poor thing.' Ace turned to look at the Doctor. 'You don't suppose it was that Viking curse, do you?'

The Doctor's expression grew dark. 'Where did you say you're meeting those other two girls?'

'Somewhere called Maidens' Point.'

'I think I'd better come with you.'

Miss Hardaker's cottage was like its owner: stony grey and heartless. Inside, the walls had been white-washed, but this only made everything seem even more cold and unwelcoming. It was certainly many years since love, warmth and affection had been visitors here.

There was a terrible look in Miss Hardaker's eyes as she stared up from her Bible to the two girls who stood in front of her. 'Maidens' Point, did you say?' Her voice was cold and threatening.

'We only want to go for a walk. Maybe have a swim,' explained Phyllis.

'I know what girls who go to Maidens' Point have in mind.' Miss Hardaker fixed the two girls with her sharp gaze. 'You will *never* go near the place, do you hear? Neither of you.'

'All right, keep your hair on,' answered Jean.

Miss Hardaker suddenly rose from her chair and angrily turned on Jean. 'You impudent child! Do you know why it's called Maidens' Point? Because when you stand on the cliffs, yu can hear the terrible, lost cries of girls who went to that place with evil in their hearts. Girls like yourselves – full of laughter. Girls who are damned *for ever*.' Miss Hardaker stared at Jean and Phyllis with frosty hatred. 'Mark my words, there's evil at Maidens' Point.'

The sea-birds screeched overhead as Ace and the Doctor stood on the shingle, staring out over the grey sea. The waves washed over the rocks with a regular rush. Ace looked out across the vast, empty horizon. 'I like watching the sea. It makes me feel so small.'

She looked down the empty shore and frowned in annoyance. 'You'd think they'd take their rubbish home with them, wouldn't you?'

'What's that you say?'

'Rubbish. People come here for a picnic and leave their rubbish behind.' Ace pointed to a small package lying in a pool.

The Doctor went over to the package to pick it up. 'I don't think this is the kind of place people come for picnics.' He looked inside the package: it contained a map of the coast, a plan of the signals camp, a photograph of Dr Judson and some documents. It was the package of sealed orders that Petrossian had dropped in his escape. The Doctor glanced through

38

the documents. 'And I don't think these were dropped by holidaymakers. Not English ones anyway.'

'Germans!' Ace's face lit up at the prospect. 'German spies!'

'Look at the lettering on the papers.'

Ace could see that the characters weren't European. 'Greek?' she suggested, thinking back to the Greek symbols she had used in maths lessons, although the idea of Greek spies struck her as a bit odd.

'Russian.'

'But the Russians were on our side during the war.'

'Precisely.'

Ace looked round. 'So where are they now?'

'More to the point, where have they come from? All the way through German-occupied Europe? Or . . .' The Doctor looked out to sea, 'or from the north, like Vikings?'

Ace looked across the waters and shivered.

The Doctor turned and began to stride back up the shingle. 'Back to the church, I think.'

'No, hang on. I said I'd meet Jean and Phyllis here.'

The Doctor looked back in annoyance. 'All right, stay here if you must.' Then he dropped his voice, and his face turned dark in warning. 'But don't go in the water.'

The chess pieces were carved into figures of Viking gods and goddesses. They stood frozen in battle – the contest between black and white forever fixed at a single moment, the clash of metal and the cry of warriors muted in the awful, silent tableau of war.

A small portrait of Adolf Hitler, Führer of the Third Reich looked out from its dull, golden frame and gazed across the miniature battlefield.

Filing cabinets stood against the wall, their drawers marked *War Office Correspondence*, *Requisitions* and *Royal Navy Standard Operations*. And there were drawers marked *German Naval Signals Traffic*, *North Atlantic Engagements* and *Berlin Central Command*.

Several old photographs hung on the wall: the pupils and staff of a public school; a portrait of a school rugby team; a young man in the uniform of a junior officer in the Royal Navy; and a ship's crew.

One face featured in all the photographs. It appeared first as a young boy with a sharp, lively face and then as a schoolboy rugby player whose expression was haunted by dark guilt. Next, the picture showed it as a young naval officer, his hard face seeming to hide terrible thoughts. And finally a lieutenant-commander's impassive expression gazed out of a photograph. The pictures were a facial history of a heart turning to stone.

The man was now a full commander, and his expression was empty as he sat at his desk. Brown folders lay open in front of him where he had been reading: *Ultima Project – Top Secret*, *German Naval Decrypts – Classified*. At the front of the desk was a small brass plate engraved with his name, Commander AH Millington. His face, however, was empty.

Who knows where the tortured thoughts of a madman may roam as they stumble through crazed memories, pursued by demon wolves and sucked down by the black undercurrents of the soul.

Ah yes, the undercurrents.

Ah yes, the wolves. The Wolves of Fenric.

The Wolf-time

An essay written twenty-seven years earlier by Millington, A. H. of Form IIC:

The Fall of the Gods

There is an end to all things, and even the gods must die. Three signs shall come before, signalling the final end. First shall be the Sword-time, three terrible years of fighting and war that will encompass the whole earth. Second shall be the Storm-time, in which unnatural storms will crack trees and split the sky. And last shall be the Wolf-time, when the great wolf Fenric who was chained by the god Tyr, will break free and darkness will engulf the world.

Then shall the gods themselves fear for their lives.

The Great Serpent shall rise from the oceans and spew its venomous fumes across all the land, killing every living thing on earth. The Dead Men's Ship shall slip its moorings and, with the evil god Loki at its helm, shall be carried by a huge wave right to Asgard, home of the gods. The Rainbow Bridge between Asgard and earth will shatter, leaving the gods trapped.

Before dawn on the morning of the final battle, the gods will gather on the battlefield of Vigrith, ready to face their final enemy. Standing against them, at the head of a mighty army of dead men, shall be the wolf Fenric, the Great Serpent and the evil Loki who was once a god. Odin, the lord of the gods, will slip away and go alone to the Great Ash Tree, where he will ask the Well of Mimir for advice. But the well shall remain silent, and Odin will return to the gods heavy-hearted, knowing that this is the end.

As the sun rises pale and weal, Heimdal, who is the gatekeeper on the Rainbow Bridge, shall feel the first faint rumble of an earthquake, and he shall raise the Gialler Horn to his lips and blow a mighty trumpet call to signal the start of battle.

Odin shall ride into battle at the head of the gods, with his warrior wife Fricka riding at one side, and Thor, the god of thunder, at the other. The mighty armies will clash, and the battlefield will thunder with the sound of death. The ancient enemies shall seek each other out, and all shall die. The great wolf Fenric shall have his revenge and devour the god Tyr, who first shackled Fenric all those centuries ago. The god Thor will hurl his magic hammer at the Great Serpent and strike it dead. But he will be touched by the serpent's final poisonous breath, and Thor will manage to walk only nine paces before he too falls dead. Loki and Heimdal will clash in scorching flames. The flames will turn into a huge fireball that shall engulf the whole of earth and heaven. The whole universe shall burn, and when the flames subside, nothing shall be left. The universe shall be as it was in the beginning: chaos.

An English master's comment has been added at

the bottom of this essay: Very good. An extraordinarily vivid piece of writing for a boy of only 12. It is almost as though young Millington really believes that these myths will come true one day.

Chronicle II

Dangerous Undercurrents

1

Nurse Crane watched anxiously as Dr Judson muttered furiously to himself.

The Ultima machine filled almost the entire room with its racks of valves and its banks of relay switches. Judson was sitting by the central section, which housed several circular rotors. He swore often and loud as he fiddled to install another rotor inside the small unit.

The door swung open, and Commander Millington strode in. 'What's going on, Judson?' he barked.

'Damn!' exclaimed Judson, as a small screw fell to the floor.

'Why the delay?' demanded Millington, striding up to Judson.

'Shut up, you idiot! Can't you see I'm busy?'

Nobody else would dare use this kind of language to a naval commander, but Judson continued with his task. The commander waited while Judson inserted another screw and fastened the rotor into place.

Dr Judson leaned back and smiled at his handiwork.

Then he remembered Millington and turned to scowl at him. 'Well, Millington. What do you want?'

'Why was this necessary? Why have you altered the rotor settings?'

'The North Atlantic U-boats have changed ciphers again,' explained Judson irritably. 'That's twice this month.'

'Can we break them?'

'It might take slightly longer. They seem to be using six rotors now, instead of five.'

'Get inside the Nazi mind, Judson.' Millington stared intently at Judson, with an insane glint in his eyes. 'Learn to think the way they think. Anticipate their thoughts. It's the only way to understand their ciphers.'

'The machine will do it, Millington.'

Dr Judson slotted the rotor unit back into position among the central racks, and plugged its wires back in. Millington leaned forward to snap shut the lock that secured the rotor unit, while Judson typed a sequence of letters into a small teletype unit attached to the machine. The valves began to glow with energy, the rotors whirred softly and finally the relay switches started to chatter.

It was like a huge monster brought slowly back to life. Dr Judson twisted round and grasped the commander's uniform to pull him closer. Judson's voice dropped to an intense whisper. 'This is just the first, Millington. There will be many more in the future – computing machines; *thinking* machines.'

Millington stared back at Judson. 'But whose thoughts will they think, Judson? Yours, or mine?'

'No-o-o! I can't! No, stop it!'

Ace and Jean fell about laughing.

45

'And stop laughing at me!' screeched Phyllis, trying hard to stop herself from laughing too. She was dangling from one of Ace's rock-climbing ropes, and hanging on to a ledge near the bottom of the cliff-face. She was only a few metres off the ground, but from her point of view it looked as dangerous as jumping off the top of St Paul's Cathedral.

'No, I can't!'

'You're always such a baby doll, Philly!' laughed Jean at the bottom.

'It's all right for you,' gasped Phyllis. 'You're five weeks older than me. You don't have as much to live for!'

'You'll be all right,' called Ace encouragingly. 'I'm holding tight on the other end of the rope. Just let go of the ledge.'

'Yeah, come on, Philly! You'll love it! It makes you feel all funny inside!'

'All right then. Get ready to catch me. And make sure I get a nice funeral!'

'Ready,' called Ace, and Phyllis let go of the ledge.

With her foot wedged tight on the free end, Ace let the rope slide quickly through her gloves.

Phyllis swung rapidly down towards the ground. 'Aaargh!' she shrieked as she felt her insides perform an impromptu double-somersault.

'Ooh! Your bloomers!' laughed Jean, seeing Phyllis's dress float upwards.

Ace tightened her grip before Phyllis reached the ground and Phyllis slowed rapidly.

Jean and Ace collapsed laughing on to the rocks as Phyllis quickly tried to restore some decorum to her wayward dress.

'Want to do it again?' called Ace

46

'No!' shrieked Phyllis. All three of them fell about in screams of laughter.

'She enjoys it really!' giggled Jean. 'You should hear what they call her at school!'

Phyllis's eyes opened wide in horror. 'Jean!'

The three girls leaned back smiling as they caught their breath.

'Your gloves are ruined,' remarked Jean.

Ace looked at her gloves. They were all ripped and torn, from the rope. Phyllis took one of Ace's hands in surprise. 'They're real leather! You're going to be in dead trouble when you get back.'

'They're just some gloves I found. They don't matter.'

'Cor, you must be rich.' Phyllis's eyes lit up as she thought of something. 'You haven't got any ciggies, have you?'

'Ciggies? Sorry, I gave up.'

Jean looked at Ace, puzzled. 'You gave up? What for?'

Ace felt a bit embarrassed. 'My mum found out.'

Jean laughed. Ace felt slightly hurt: there was something sharp and wounding about the older girl's personality.

'Your uncle doesn't mind you coming down here by yourself?' asked Phyllis. With her soft brown eyes and round smiling face, Phyllis seemed a warmer person.

'Who? Oh, you mean the Professor. No, he's OK really.'

Jean laughed contemptuously. 'The old witch said we oughtn't to come here.'

'There's evil in the water!' laughed the two girls in unison. They looked at each other, smiling and obviously thinking the same thought.

47

'Come on!' exclaimed Jean, and the two evacuees grabbed their satchels and ran off. Ace jumped up and ran after.

A tall, jagged boulder that had split away from the cliff provided a natural screen from the rest of the shore. Jean and Phyllis disappeared behind it. They pulled swimming costumes and towels from their satchels.

'What you doing?' asked Ace uncertainly.

Jean was unbuttoning the front of her dress. 'What's it look like, dummy? We're going for a swim, of course. Come on.'

'I can't. I haven't got anything to wear.'

'There's no one about. No one'll see you. Come on.' Jean had already undressed, discarding her clothes where they fell. She reached for her swimming costume. She saw Ace watching her, and smiled lazily.

Ace looked quickly away. 'Nah, swimming's stupid.'

'Come on! Don't be such a baby doll!' laughed Jean as she pulled one strap of the costume up over her arm.

'Yeah, it'll be lovely and warm,' agreed Phyllis, stepping into her own swimming costume. 'Don't you want to feel the waves rushing all over you?'

She was right. The sun was coming out, and a swim would be so much fun. But Ace couldn't forget the Doctor's warning.

'What about that?' Ace pointed to an old sign. It read: No Swimming – Dangerous Undercurrents.

'You're just a baby doll,' mocked Jean.

'Don't take any notice of that,' urged Phyllis. 'They say things like that just so's you can't enjoy yourself. Don't worry. Once you're in the water, it'll be great.'

48

'Come on, Philly. Don't wait for her. She can stay and play with her bucket and spade, like a baby doll.'

The two girls ran laughing down the beach and into the water, but Ace didn't follow them. She watched them splashing in the shallows, throwing water at each other. They shrieked as they waded in deeper.

'Ooh, it feels all funny, Jean! I think I've got some seaweed wrapped round my legs!'

'There's a big wave coming, Philly! Get ready for it!'

'Yeah!' screamed Phyllis in delight as the wave broke over them both and left them laughing breathlessly.

'Stupid,' Ace muttered to herself. She turned to go and find the Doctor, but deep down she longed to go into the water. She wanted to laugh and splash and fight; she wanted to feel the waves crash about her and feel the sea rushing all over her body; she wanted to float peacefully, as the warm waters gently caressed her. But the Doctor's words had frightened her and she was scared that some kind of black sea creature might grab at her from deep down.

She looked back. Jean and Phyllis were bobbing happily among the waves, but Ace had missed her chance.

Mr Wainwright was absorbed reading an old record book, sitting at the table in the vestry. His face was full of misgivings.

The Doctor coughed.

Mr Wainwright quickly shut the book and looked round. 'I'm terribly sorry, Doctor. I didn't hear you come in.'

'Possibly not.'

'What can I do for you?'

'I'd like to know the answer.'

Mr Wainwright looked anxious. 'I'm afraid I don't understand.'

'Yes, afraid. But afraid of what? Is it those Viking inscriptions – the curse?'

'Doctor, there are some questions better left unanswered.'

'But it's too late, isn't it?' The Doctor looked at the old record book. 'Someone has already translated the inscriptions, haven't they?'

'It's probably all nonsense. Some records my grandfather made when he was vicar of St Jude's at the end of the last century.' Mr Wainwright reluctantly handed the book to the Doctor. The young vicar's heart was heavy. 'He translated the Viking inscriptions. I wish to heaven he never had.'

The Doctor opened the book and began to read the carefully formed handwriting.

We hoped to return to the North Way, carrying home the oriental treasures from the Silk Lands in the east, but the dark curse follows our dragonship.

The Doctor turned on a few pages, and read some more of the faded ink.

Black fog turned day into night, and the fingers of death reached out from the waters to reclaim the treasure we have stolen.

I carve these stones in memory of Jorun and Torkel, courageous friends who died in the Baltic waters.

I carve these stones in the memory of Asmund,

Rognvald, and Halfdan, brave warriors who died in the North Sea.

I carve these stones in memory of Yngvar, my only brother, slain by the curse.

We have sought haven in Northumbria and taken refuge at a place called Maidens' Bay, but the curse of the treasure has followed us to this place.

The Doctor looked up at Mr Wainwright. 'Maidens' Bay?'

'It's called Maidens' Point now.'

The Doctor was suddenly anxious. 'I've just left Ace there.'

'Yeah, but I'm back now, aren't I? What you got there, Professor?'

The Doctor turned in relief to see Ace sauntering through the door. 'It's a translation of the Viking inscriptions,' he explained. 'And I've just noticed something.'

'What's that?'

'Something I just read.' He turned back a couple of pages. 'Let me see. Yes, here we are: We hoped to return to the North Way, carrying home the oriental treasure.' The Doctor then pulled the package of Russian documents from his pocket. 'Now listen to this. Vozravschayetes v Norwegioo s sakrovischem.'

Ace looked at him blankly. 'I only did French O level.'

'It means: return to Norway with the treasure,' the Doctor explained excitedly as a broad smile spread across his face. 'Let's see how Dr Judson's getting along, shall we?'

Jean and Phyllis raced up the beach and collapsed panting on the rocks by their clothes. Phyllis lay back and stretched out in the warm sun. Tiny rivulets of water trickled across her glistening skin and collected in small puddles on the rocks beneath her. 'That was great,' she sighed.

'What are we going to do about drying our things?' asked Jean, peeling off her wet swimming costume.

Phyllis sat up and took her towel to dry her arms and legs. 'What about behind those bushes at the back of the cottage?'

'OK. We'll have to hide them in our room until there's a chance to sneak out with them.'

'The towels don't matter. We can just say they're still wet from this morning.' Phyllis stripped off her own costume and began to dry the rest of her body.

Jean looked at Phyllis, with a gleam in her eye. 'You know, we could get in trouble if someone comes along and finds us like this!'

Phyllis quickly held her towel in front of her, trying to cover herself. 'Jean!' she giggled.

'Hurry up!' laughed Jean, pulling her dress down over her head.

'I don't know why I let you talk me into doing these things. You're always getting me into trouble.'

''Cause it's a laugh, that's why. And anyway, if it weren't for me, you'd still be a baby doll – know what I mean?' Jean smiled slyly. Phyllis turned bright red and Jean laughed. 'Come on, get your knickers on, and do my legs for me.'

Jean rummaged in her satchel while Phyllis struggled into her dress. 'Here you are, gormless,' she said, handing Phyllis a black make-up pencil and turning away. She brushed out her damp hair, while Phyllis drew two even lines down the back of Jean's legs – perfect imitations of the seams of a pair of nylon stockings.

'Hold still, will you?' scolded Phyllis, as Jean shook out her long blonde hair.

'Make me look like Lana Turner.'

'You mean Betty Grable,' corrected Phyllis. 'She's the actress with long legs. Lana Turner's the one who always wears sweaters.'

'You spend too much time looking at the screen. I've got better things to do in the back row of the pictures. Hey, look at that.'

Jean pointed at something that lay among the rocks. It looked like a cluster of small metal objects – a coin, a nail and a small hinge – that were welded together with coral. The metal wasn't at all rusty and it still glittered bright and shiny beneath the rainbow hues of the coral.

'What is it?' asked Phyllis.

'I don't know.' Jean reached to pick it up. As she did so, she felt a slight tingling sensation over her entire body – as though all her skin were sparkling. 'Ooh, it feels funny. Sort of tickly. Here.'

She gave it to Phyllis. As soon as it touched Phyllis's skin, she felt the strange feeling as well, like a light, early morning frost over all her skin. It sent a shiver up her spine.

'Oh, it's like electric!' Phyllis quickly dropped the strange coral object.

Jean reached to pick it up again, but Phyllis stopped her. 'No, leave it. I don't like it.'

Jean shrugged her shoulders. 'It's just a bit of junk.' She began to bundle her things into her satchel. 'Come on. We don't want the old bag to be worrying.'

'Dr Judson, there's something here that might interest you.'

Judson looked round from the blackboard where he

was scribbling, and saw the Doctor and Ace marching through the door of his office. The Doctor held a large record book.

'What's that?' demanded Dr Judson.

'A nineteenth-century translation of the Viking inscriptions, written down by Mr Wainwright's grandfather.'

'Let me see.' Dr Judson propelled his wheelchair rapidly across the room, and took the old book. He read it at the page where it fell open.

Night is the time of the evil curse, and no man is safe alone.

The waters are the most dangerous. The dark evil lies waiting in the sea. It has followed the treasure we stole. We cannot see the evil, but we know that it is there: beneath the surface, beyond seeing, but it is there.

And one by one, our crew is being killed.

Dr Judson looked up at the Doctor. 'You were right to bring this to me. I think it would be better if I were to keep it.'

Trofimov lay flat among the rocks. Through the sunsight of his Tokarev, he watched the two girls approaching. His finger tightened on the trigger.

'No closer,' he muttered quietly, but Jean and Phyllis continued to approach, laughing with each other.

Trofimov watched them. As Phyllis looked up, he saw her face, round and smiling, with her warm brown hair – and he thought of Irena. He remembered Irena the first time he saw her, just before the war. She was a girl then, almost nineteen, and she had laughing brown eyes and soft chestnut hair. The photograph of her in his pocket was only black-and-white, but she still seemed to be smiling to him with warm, brown eyes.

He looked through the gunsight once more. 'Please,' he murmured, 'no closer.'

With a shriek of laughter, the two girls suddenly turned and went off in a different direction. Trofimov breathed a sigh of relief and relaxed his finger on the trigger. He watched them until they had disappeared down the path to the village, then he got up.

The rocks crunched beneath his boots as he hurried along the shore to the cracked boulder where Jean and Phyllis had changed. It would give him good cover while he kept watch on the shore. He would be well hidden, but it was easy for him to look out through cracks where the boulder had shattered.

Something on the ground caught his eye. It was the strange coral object which lay where Phyllis had dropped it. Trofimov reached to pick it up.

As soon as he touched it, he felt a shiver run over his skin and up his spine. It was like the kiss of a dead woman.

For a moment, an image of Irena came into his mind. This time, however, she didn't have warm, brown eyes: they were a piercing black that stood out sharply from her deathly white face with its rich, blood-red lips that laughed mockingly.

Trofimov quickly shut the image from his mind and turned towards the sea. He hurled the evil object with all his strength.

It glittered as it spun through the air before it hit the surface of the water and was swallowed up. Trofimov turned away and shivered again at the memory of the dead woman's mocking laugh.

2

No entry to unauthorized personnel read the notice on the door.

'That probably means us,' smiled the Doctor. He pushed open the door. Inside, a dozen or more young women in the smart, navy blue uniforms of the WRNS were sitting at trestle-tables. Each of them had a large radio receiver and they were all wearing headphones.

'I never knew they had personal stereos in 1943,' muttered Ace.

'They're listening to coded German radio messages.'

Now that the Doctor mentioned it, Ace noticed the faint sound of Morse code coming from the headsets.

A young woman with a cheery face glanced up from the notepad where she was copying down the transmission and saw the Doctor and Ace. She smiled at them and took off her headphones. 'Are you looking for someone?'

'Just being nosy,' explained the Doctor. 'We're from the War Office.'

'Sorry, no one warned us. We're the girls. I'm Kathleen Dudman.'

One or two of the Wrens smiled and nodded to the Doctor, but Ace was peering round in curiosity. Kathleen noticed, and asked if she could help.

'No, it's OK. I just thought I heard a baby somewhere.'

Kathleen suddenly began to fidget awkwardly. 'A baby?' she laughed. 'No, not on a naval camp.'

The baby gurgled again; Kathleen's face reddened

with guilt. Ace peered under the table where the sound was coming from. There, lying in a baby basket, she saw the most delightful little thing imaginable. 'Cor, look, Professor! It's a sprog!' She pulled the basket out from under the table.

Kathleen looked anxiously at the Doctor. 'It's not what you think, sir. I mean . . . only for today . . . I couldn't leave her by herself.'

The Doctor suddenly understood. Kathleen thought she was going to get into trouble for bringing her baby into a top secret naval camp. 'Don't worry,' he smiled, 'I think we can bend the regulations just this once. Just as long as you can promise me she's isn't a German spy, sent to discover the secret of British nappies.'

'Oh no, sir!' laughed Kathleen in relief.

Ace was still absorbed by the little bundle on the floor. The baby was gurgling happily, and Ace's eyes were wide in delight. 'Aren't you the most cuddlesome creature in the whole wide world?' she whispered. Then she looked up at Kathleen. 'Can I pick her up, and hold her a bit?'

'You'll have to excuse my assistant,' explained the Doctor. 'She's from Perivale.'

'That's all right. Of course you can hold her.'

'Ace!'

Kathleen knelt down, and helped Ace pick the baby up, which was a bit trickier than Ace had imagined, what with all the arms and legs that babies have. But soon Ace stood up holding the little baby. She felt it snuggle warmly in her arms. She saw the large brown eyes smiling up at their new mum. Ace's heart melted.

'Oh, she's beautiful. And look at her little fingernails. They're so tiny – so perfect and tiny.'

'Every one a heartbreaker,' muttered the Doctor, who was feeling a bit left out.

Ace looked to Kathleen. 'What's her name?'

'Audrey.'

Ace's face fell. 'Oh.'

'What's the matter? Don't you like it?'

'My mum was called Audrey.' Ace's voice was bitter, and her embrace stiffened. Baby Audrey protested slightly with a fretful sound, so Ace held her out for Kathleen to take. 'I think she wants to go back to you.'

Kathleen took the little baby and began to rock her gently.

At that moment, the door opened and Millington strode in. Kathleen's cheerfulness quickly evaporated; the Wrens who had been looking at the baby hurriedly returned to their work.

Millington stared at the baby in Kathleen's arms. 'Dudman, I gave clear instructions that the baby was not to remain on camp.' His voice was cold and unfriendly.

Kathleen suddenly felt quite alone and frightened. 'Yes, sir.'

'Well?' demanded the commander.

'I thought she could stay with my cousin, sir,' explained Kathleen. 'But their cottage is too small.'

'Twenty-four hours, Dudman, or I shall have you dismissed from service.'

'Yes, sir.'

Ace was growing more and more angry at this man's attitude. She started to march up to him. 'Here, who do you think you are, armpit?'

But the Doctor grabbed her by the collar and pulled her back. 'Shh, not now,' he muttered as he bustled her quickly out of the door.

Millington barely seemed to have noticed the minor commotion behind him as he looked round the roomful of women. His expression began to twist unpleasantly. Women – they even smelled different.

The Doctor bundled Ace out of the hut and out of sight round the corner. She was annoyed at this treatment. 'Why didn't you let me sort him out, Professor?'

'Because there are more effective ways. Look.'

Ace followed the Doctor's gaze. She saw Millington emerge from the hut and stride off towards Dr Judson's office. The Doctor smiled. 'Come on,' he whispered.

'Where are we off to?'

'I thought we might have a quick rummage through the commander's office while he's busy.'

The Doctor disappeared in the direction of Millington's hut. Ace hurried along behind him.

'A *girl*?' demanded Millington. 'From the War Office?' He peered intensely at Dr Judson.

'Yes, highly unusual, I must agree. But she's a genius. She understands the logic diagrams. They're both mathematical specialists.'

'You fool! They're from Bletchley! The Army has sent them to discover the details of Ultima.' The commander began to pace about Judson's office, thinking aloud. 'We shall have to kill them. We cannot allow the army to discover the secrets of your work.'

Dr Judson bristled at Millington's outburst. 'They're not from Bletchley. I've made enquiries. They've never heard of him there.' Then Judson's eyes flared mischievously as he remembered the old record book. 'And they've found a translation of those Viking inscriptions.'

Millington turned and stared at Dr Judson. He saw the old book that the cripple was holding out to him and suddenly his courage froze: he hardly dared take the records and read them. The ancient Viking carvings – secrets from more than a thousand years ago – were the reason for Millington's insistence that the Ultima research should be carried out at an insignificant signals camp near the Yorkshire coast. It was so that he might learn the dark knowledge of the inscriptions in the local church. But now that Dr Judson finally offered him the answers, Millington was suddenly afraid.

Judson's smile taunted Millington like the devil Mephistopheles had taunted Faust. Take it, it seemed to say. Take the knowledge you desire; learn the dark secrets.

Millington reached out and took the book.

The book fell open near the end. Millington read the words.

I warn of the day when the Earth shall fall asunder, and all of heaven too. The Wolves of Fenric shall return for their treasure, and then shall the Dark Evil rule eternally.

A chill shiver whispered through Millington's soul. 'This is it,' he murmured. 'The final battle between the gods and the beasts. It's now, Judson! The curse of Fenric!'

He looked up.

His eyes were filled with horror.

* * *

60

Millington's office was empty as the Doctor cautiously opened the door and peered inside. Ace followed him in, and he closed the door. 'You keep watch out of the window, Ace. Look for anyone heading this way.'

'Brill! This is well exciting!' Ace hopped over to the window, and crouched down out of sight.

The Doctor gazed round the room. The rows of filing cabinets, the portrait of Hitler, the golden German eagle. He'd seen it all somewhere before, but where? Then he remembered.

'Extraordinary!'

'What've you found?'

'This whole office. It's a perfect replica of the German naval cipher room in Berlin, even the files. They're arranged identically.'

Ace looked round. 'You mean Commander Millington's a spy?'

'No, no. I think even the nitwits in the British secret service might get a bit suspicious about portraits of Adolf Hitler lying around!' smiled the Doctor. 'No, Millington's trying to get inside the German mind and learn to think the way the Germans think so he can understand how they construct their ciphers. But he's done it so perfectly. It's extraordinary.' The Doctor looked round. 'What else have we got?'

He saw the photographs hanging on the wall and looked carefully at them. 'Well, well, well. The old school tie.'

'Who are they?' Ace crept over to join the Doctor. She peered at the sepia brown photos.

'This one.' The Doctor indicated a portrait of a school rugby team. 'Recognize any of the faces?'

As Ace peered at the row of faces; she immediately recognized the young Millington, with his dark, guilty eyes. 'It's the commander,' she said.

'Very good. Anyone else?'

Ace scanned further along the row of faces, and she was surprised to recognize a second expression, with its fiery, greedy eyes. 'Dr Judson!'

'Yes, and before he was injured. Bit of a coincidence, don't you think?'

Millington strode across the camp towards his office, but his mind was trapped struggling in the memories of more than twenty years earlier. Memories of a few split seconds that replayed endlessly in his mind.

The cold mud of a ruby pitch. The shouts and calls of adolescent young men as they ran and chased. The expression Millington saw on Judson's face as Judson smiled across to one of the other players, a tall, blond boy with clear blue eyes and a strong body. The sharp, stabbing jealousy that surged through Millington. The black anger that filled him as he ran towards Judson. The hatred, as he drove his shoulder hard in Judson's back. The cracking sound – the awful cracking sound – as Judson's body bent backwards and his spine fractured. The expression in Judson's face, an expression from hell, as he lay paralysed in the mud.

'I'm sorry,' wept Millington. 'I didn't mean . . .'

Judson looked up from the hospital bed, and Millington saw the answer in Judson's black eyes. *You're mine now!* said the eyes. *Mine for ever.*

'Look, more Vikings.'

Ace had found the Viking chess game. The Doctor came to look at it.

'Why's everyone around here so interested in Vikings, Professor?'

'Yes, I wonder.'

There was a sound at the door. The Doctor and Ace froze as the handle turned and the door opened.

Millington walked in, but his face was empty. He went to sit behind his desk, passing right by the Doctor and Ace without seeing them.

'What's happened to him?' hissed Ace.

'Shh.'

The Doctor crept towards Millington, and examined the commander's expression. 'He seems to be in some kind of trance.'

Something stirred in the commander's mind. 'No,' he murmured restlessly.

'What is it?' whispered the Doctor. 'What can you see?'

Millington's haunted face reflected images too horrible to describe.

'What is it?' urged the Doctor. 'Tell me, Millington. Tell me what you see.'

'Maidens' Point,' murmured the commander.

'What is it? What is there at Maidens' Point?'

'Undercurrents . . . bringing things to the surface.'

'What are they bringing to the surface?'

Mine for ever.

'No.' Millington's eyes stared in horror.

'What can you see? You must tell me.'

'No.'

'Tell me!'

'No!' With a cry, Millington looked up. He was confounded. Where was he? Who were these people? He looked at the Doctor. 'What do you want?'

The Doctor smiled and politely raised his hat. 'Terribly sorry, commander. Wrong office. Come along, Ace. Dr Judson's office must be in the other hut.'

63

The Doctor turned quickly and hurried out, pulling Ace with him.

The Doctor scrambled over the rocks at Maidens' Point; Ace hurried to keep up.

'I'm confused, Professor. Why was he going on about Maidens' Point? I mean, does he know about the Russians or doesn't he? What's going on?'

'My guess is that we'll find out down here. We must have missed something when we found those Russian papers. Have a look around. Over there.' The Doctor gestured to the other side of some rocks.

Ace went to investigate. 'What are we looking for? I mean, is it big, or . . .' Her voice tailed off, and she looked down in horror. 'Professor.'

'What have you found?' The Doctor hurried to join her.

Lying in a rock pool was the dead body of Petrossian. Knifeblade cuts criss-crossed his body, but there was no blood on the rocks.

The Doctor knelt down beside the dead body, and closed its eyes. 'Yes, not very pleasant. But what's he holding?'

The Doctor prised open Petrossian's clenched fist. Inside, an old-fashioned iron key was coated with lustrous coral. The Doctor took the object and slipped it into his pocket.

The clicks of several Tokarev rifles made the Doctor and Ace look up.

They were surrounded by soldiers in a uniform which the Doctor recognized as that of the Red Army Special Missions Brigade. The commandos raised their guns to shoot.

'No!' commanded Trofimov. 'No shooting. We don't want to attract attention.'

He reached out and picked up a heavy rock. 'We must kill them silently.'

The Doctor looked round desperately. 'Do you have the faintest idea what's going on here – the danger you're all in?' He tried to plead with the stony Russian faces. 'Do you really think we killed him?'

Trofimov looked coldly at the Doctor. 'It doesn't matter whether you killed him or you didn't. You found him, so you know too much. You die.'

'We know more than you think.' The Doctor returned the Russian's cold stare. 'Vozravschayetes v Norwegioo s sakrovischem.'

The commandos were startled to hear the Doctor's words. Suddenly Ace remembered. These were the words he'd read to her from the Russian documents: return to Norway with the treasure.

Corporal Vershinin quickly turned to the sergeant. 'Kill them, Trofimov. Kill them now.'

But Vershinin was young – barely 18 – with an idealistic fervour that glowed in his eyes. The sergeant was older and more experienced, and he was interested in this stranger who spoke Russian. 'No. We take them back to Captain Sorin. I'm sure he'd like to hear them speak a little Russian too.'

But Trofimov didn't smile as he spoke. There was something wrong with this mission. Too many people were being killed. He couldn't explain it to the youthful Vershinin. After all, that's what happens in war – people get killed. But it was beginning to feel wrong.

Dr Judson was also gripped by dark thoughts as he finished reading the old translation of the Viking inscriptions, the final words carved centuries ago by a man who knew he would soon die.

I am the only one left alive now.

I raise these stones to my wife Astrid. May she forgive my sin.

The day grows dark, and I sense the evil curse rising from the sea. I now understand what the curse of Fenric seeks: the treasures from the Silk Lands in the east.

I have heard the treasures whisper in my dreams. I have heard the magic words that will release great powers. I must not let it happen. I shall bury the treasures for ever.

Tonight I shall die, and the secret words shall die with me.

What were the secret words? And what were the great powers these words would release? And what was the sin? He said he was going to die, and he wanted his wife to forgive him. What had he done?

Judson felt cold. He looked around, but there was no draught. This was a black, unnatural chill – the chill of evil.

Judson knew he should stop now. There was something dangerous here, and he should leave it hidden where it had been buried for a thousand years. But he wanted to *know*. He was a scientist, driven by the great thirst for knowledge. He had to see these great powers for himself, just once. These would be the chains he would throw around Millington's soul.

The crypt was dark. Along the wall stood the rune stones, faint marks carved more than a thousand years ago. And at the end of the wall, the final stone was empty.

A blank page waiting for a message.

And the invisible finger moved across the stone.

Marks began to appear. In Viking letters even older than the others, the final message carved itself in the shadows.

Here it is, Dr Judson! Here are the dark words you desire!

Come and read them.

Document II

The Curse of the Flask

From The Saga of Hrothulf, *translated by Graeme Wilson (Oxford Polytechnic Press, 1977)*:

Listen.

On the Eve of his Wedding, *Hrothulf* held a great
    feast,
and as the sun went down, he summoned the
    Poet
to tell them a tale suitable for the occasion.
So the Poet stood up, and started to recite   5
the tale of *Hemming* and the curse of the treasure.

When *Hengest* was old, he was blessed with a son,
whom he named *Oslaf*. And when Oslaf grew
to be a man, he became a merchant traveller.
Many times, he journeyed across the seas   10
to the land of the Polacks*, and from thence
over land and down river he travelled,
until he reached the great city of Constantinople.

11 *land of the Polacks* ie Poland.

There, he would bargain with the market-sellers, and buy
fine treasures brought from the Silk Lands in the East.   *15*
Then he would return to the Svear* with his merchandise,
and always he gave one treasure to his lord *Halfdeane*
(who was grandfather to our own lord Hrothulf)
as a gift and sign of Oslaf's allegiance.

So it happened that Oslaf was in Constantinople   *20*
when he heard of a treasure for sale, an old flask,
worthless and dirty, but the market-seller told Oslaf
that great riches were contained inside. And Oslaf,
thinking this would make a fine gift for Halfdeane,
bought the flask and added it to his merchandise.   *25*
But the market-seller never told Oslaf
that the flask was cursed with evil and death.

As Oslaf and his men returned, they travelled through
the country of Transylvania, full of green forests
and blue rivers. But as they slept one night,   *30*
a black fog, not like anything they had seen before,
crept from the forests, and in the morning two men

16 *Svear* A large tribe dominating central Sweden. (The modern Swedish name for the country, *Sverige*, is a corruption of the Old Norse word *Sviariki*, 'kingdom of the Svear'.)

lay dead, their mouths open and their faces
  white.
Oslaf continued the journey homeward with
  heavy heart,
but the curse now followed them. Each night   *35*
the fog would gather, and each morning
more men lay dead. Soon they reached the
  dolphins'
great playing-field, the Baltic sea, and they
hoped to be quickly safe at home.
But fierce pirates from the North way* now
  attacked   *40*
their ship, and soon Oslaf and all his men
dined silent with the dolphins.

The pirate captain, who was that terrifying
  warrior
Hemming (of whom other poets speak in fearful
  tongues),
took all of Oslaf's treasure for his own.   *45*
But the dark curse followed Hemming's dragon
  ship,
and as night fell, the black fog shrouded the ship,
and two men died. Each night, more men
would die, so Hemming sought refuge in a
  Northumbrian bay.

For a time, no more strange deaths occurred,   *50*
and Hemming took his men ashore to plunder
  and rob.
The village they attacked was poor, and had no
  gold,
but Hemming saw a beautiful girl, named *Ingelda*

40 *the North way* ie Norway.

70

because her hair shone red like burnished gold,
    and he said,
'She is your greatest treasure. I shall take her
    instead.'   55
He quickly forgot his wife Astrid, waiting at
    home in the North,
and soon Ingelda gave birth to a daughter, whom
    Hemming named
Wulf-aga, because she had the shining eyes of a
    wolf.

And now the curse returned, to punish his sin
with Ingelda. The black fog swirled   60
round the bay once more, cloaking the dragon
    ship
in death. Finally, all the crew were dead
except Hemming, Ingelda, and their child Wulf-
    aga.
Hemming turned to Ingelda and said,
'The black fog is following the flask I stole.   65
It will kill us all. For the sake of you
and our daughter, I shall hide the flask
where no one can find it.'

That day, Hemming buried all his warrior-
    friends
and carved stones to place over their graves.   70
Then he kissed Ingelda farewell and said,
'You must go now, and take Wulf-aga to safety.'
When the girl and their daughter had left,
Hemming hid the flask where no one would find
    it.
As night fell, he prayed for his soul and for his
    sins.   75

The black fog reached out from the waters, and
   soon
Hemming lay dead with his friends.
But the flask lay hidden where the curse could
   not
reach it, for the warriors' graves were holy
   places,
and the curse could not tread there.   *80*

And as he finished his tale, the Poet looked
   round
and said, 'Let all the warriors here take warning
of the fate that lies waiting if you abandon
your wife for a beautiful village girl.
For surely Hemming paid dear for this sin.'   *85*

And great Hrothulf swore that he would heed
   the lesson
of the Poet's story, and remain faithful
to the bride he would take the next day,
and a mighty cheer rang through the halls.

Chronicle III

Weapons within Weapons
Death within Death

1

The Doctor tried one final time to make the Russian captain understand. 'If you attack the base, you'll walk straight into a trap. And if you stay here in the cave, you'll die just like your comrade outside.'

Sorin looked at the Doctor. 'And if I let you go, you'll betray us.'

'You must trust us.'

Sorin laughed.

'You must,' pleaded the Doctor. 'It's the only way, if you want to stop the evil that's killing your men.'

Suddenly, a cry echoed from the back of the cave. The Doctor spun round, and saw Gayev lying on the ground. The commando was pale and covered in cuts, just like the dead body that Ace had found.

Ace saw the terror in Gayev's eyes. 'What happened to him?'

Trofimov turned on her. '*You* tell *us*. His mind's in pieces.'

The Doctor stepped towards Gayev. 'Whatever it

was that killed the other one, he's seen it.' He knelt down by the terrified commando, and spoke softly, 'Tell us what you saw. Tell us.'

'This is useless,' interrupted young Vershinin. But Sorin motioned him to be quiet.

The Doctor's voice was calm and reassuring. 'Think back . . . Maidens' Point. Think back to the sea . . . the undercurrents. What was it? What did you see?'

Young Vershinin's impatience was too much, and he interrupted again. 'This is a waste of time. Anyone can see he'll never speak another word.'

But Sorin looked angrily at him, and Vershinin fell silent.

'The undercurrents . . . deep down. What can you see?' The Doctor's soothing voice began gently to tease apart the man's tightly knotted thoughts. Gayev's eyes opened wide in fear as the Doctor took him back through the haunted memories, back down into the dark waters.

'What is it?' The Doctor's words were soft and gentle. 'What do you see?'

Suddenly, Gayev looked straight at the Doctor. Their eyes met. Gayev opened his mouth, and tried to speak. But the words wouldn't come, just a moan of pain and fear.

But the Doctor understood. 'You want to show me something. What is it?'

Gayev slowly lifted an arm to the Doctor and opened his clenched fist. The Doctor looked down. In Gayev's trembling hand was a small object – part of an old iron hinge, but shiny bright and coated in a lustrous pink coral.

The Doctor reached into his pocket and drew out the coral-coated iron key he had found in the dead commando's hand. He held it up for Gayev to see.

Gayev's eyes filled with terror, and he screamed out. It was a scream that cut right through the soul – the abject terror of a man trapped in a cell with no door and no light.

The Doctor quickly put his finger to the terrified man's temples, and reached down into the man's mind. Gayev immediately fell into a deep dreamless sleep.

The cave was silent as the Doctor turned to look at the Russian captain.

'I believe you,' said Sorin quietly. 'We'll delay our attack until you and the girl both return.'

'This is madness!' protested Vershinin.

Sorin turned to look at the young commando. 'We're playing for high stakes. Victory goes to those who take the greatest risk.'

Dr Judson scribbled angrily in the cold gloom of the crypt. 'Why didn't he translate the final inscription? It's always the family idiot who takes the cloth!'

Nurse Crane shivered. 'I don't like it down here.'

'Then go away.' The final inscription – he must know what it said. He must copy it down and find out what it meant.

'Don't you feel the cold? It's like winter – most unsuitable for an invalid.'

'Shut up, Crane.'

'Come on, let's have you back in the warm.'

Nurse Crane began to lift Judson and carry him back up to his wheelchair in the vestry.

'What? No, leave me! You stupid woman! You . . .'

'Language, please,' admonished Nurse Crane. 'Remember there's a lady present.'

* * *

'Those two girls must be found and punished.' Miss Hardaker's voice hung like frost in the cottage, as she stared at the Doctor and Ace.

'We weren't causing any trouble,' Ace tried to explain. 'We were just having a lark.'

Miss Hardaker's frosty eyes turned on Ace.

'Young lady, they have deliberately defied my instructions and they must be punished.' She turned on the Doctor. 'I'm surprised that you allow your niece to play on the cliffs. Any kind of accident might happen. I'm going to call the Home Guard to find those wretched girls.'

Miss Hardaker reached for the telephone and lifted the handset.

'Professor!' hissed Ace. 'The Russians!'

The Doctor quickly stepped forward and pressed the cradle of the telephone. The handset went dead. 'No, don't do that, Miss Hardaker.'

'Those two girls have got to be found.'

'Quite,' agreed the Doctor. 'But I don't think we need waste the Home Guard's time. Not when there's a war on. Leave it to us. Come along, Ace.' The Doctor pulled Ace towards the door. 'Don't worry, Miss Hardaker. We'll find them.'

The Doctor dragged Ace out, politely raising his hat to Miss Hardaker, and closed the door.

Miss Hardaker turned back to the telephone, and tapped on the cradle until a voice answered in the earpiece.

'Yes. I'd like to be connected to the Home Guard, please.'

Millington stared at Dr Judson's copy of the new inscription. What did it mean?

He turned to Judson. 'Use the Ultima machine! Use the machine to translate the inscriptions.'

Dr Judson's eyes sparkled black. He knew Millington couldn't resist the lure of the Viking mystery. 'But what about the German signals?' he protested innocently.

'Use the machine!' commanded Millington.

2

'Ooh, I love men in uniform!' called Jean in laughter.

'Don't they look strong!' mocked Phyllis.

In fact the six men looked anything but strong. They were from the local Home Guard unit, and had been sent to search for the two girls. Their uniforms either hung like an oversize sack on a wire clothes-hanger or were bursting at the seams, trying to contain a lazy, overweight body.

'I certainly feel safe knowing that they're protecting England!' laughed Jean. 'The Germans'll take one look and die laughing!'

The Home Guard men shuffled in embarrassment. The fit young men from the village were all in the regular army; these older men also wanted to help defend their country against the Nazis, so they had joined the Home Guard.

'We'll have less of your cheek,' replied the Home Guard corporal. 'You two are in serious trouble with Miss Hardaker for coming down here in the first place.'

'We can look after ourselves.' Jean's fierce blue eyes defied the corporal to contradict her. 'Come on, Philly. There's no one here worth bothering with.'

Arm in arm, the two girls marched off towards the village.

The Home Guard patrol shambled away towards Maidens' Point to continue defending their country from the might of the German menace.

Half a mile away, hidden among the rocks of Maidens' Point, young Vershinin watched the Home Guard patrol through his binoculars. He gestured to Trofimov, who turned his binoculars and saw the Home Guard approaching along the shore.

'Fetch the captain,' whispered Trofimov.

'I thought we were going to look for Jean and Phyllis.' Ace's voice echoed in the empty church.

'We are looking.' The Doctor smiled. 'Well, they *could* have come to the church.' He looked round curiously. 'Why do I feel there's something different about this place?'

'Yeah, it doesn't even look like a church.'

'What do you mean?'

'Well, from the outside, it looks more like a small fortress.'

'No, no. I mean different since we were last here. I think it's time I had a proper look at those inscriptions.'

In the dismal churchyard, Mr Wainwright stood silent before a gravestone.

Hannah Mary Wainwright
Born 13 May 1898
Died 31 September 1920

William Wainwright
Born 16 March 1868
Died 8 March 1935

Grace Wainwright
Born 22 November 1871
Died 28 March 1939

George Frederick Wainwright
Born 23 February 1892
Died 1 June 1941

There was no 31st day of September. Not in 1920 nor any other year. He had been born on the 29th, and his mother had died the next day, on the 30th. But he had left the error, just as his father had left it for more than twenty years.

His father had shown him old photographs of a beautiful young woman whose bright, laughing eyes blazed full of life in the fading pictures. 'She was a rare one, your mother. She was an angel even before she died.'

Who were you, Hannah Mary Wainwright? he thought.

Then he looked down at the final inscription: George Frederick Wainwright. He remembered his father's funeral less than two years ago. The church was full of villagers who had come to pay their respects to a dear friend. The bishop spoke of a man full of love, full of warmth.

Why did you leave me so soon? I wasn't ready. I'm too young.

Mr Wainwright was lost in his memories. He didn't notice Millington striding down the path towards tbe church door.

'Can you hear any noises from behind the walls?' Ace crept into the crypt behind the Doctor.

'Not a thing.'

79

'I definitely heard them.'

The Doctor was peering at the Viking inscriptions. He pointed to the final stone. 'Look at this. What do you notice?'

Ace knelt down, and examined the carvings. At first, the end stone seemed just like all the others, then she noticed it was slightly different. 'Oh yes, it's written in a slightly different alphabet from the others.'

'Yes?' The Doctor obviously wanted her to tell him something more.

'Um, let's see.' Ace compared the final stone with the others. 'This alphabet doesn't use as many letters.'

'And?'

Ace tried to remember what the Doctor had said to Dr Judson earlier in the morning. 'And . . . and that means it's older than all the others.'

'And?' The Doctor was sounding a bit like an impatient teacher.

'Um . . .' But Ace couldn't think of anything else. Her face fell. 'Don't know.'

'And it wasn't here this morning.'

'What? But these inscriptions have been here a thousand years!'

At the top of the stairs, the vestry door opened.

'Quick, hide!' whispered the Doctor. He extinguished the lamp and pulled Ace round a corner and into the shadows.

A heavy footstep descended the stone stairs and the yellow glow of another oil lamp grew closer.

The footsteps reached the bottom of the stairs and echoed across the stone floor. Ace held her breath and watched the light of the oil lamp getting closer. She shut her eyes tight, like a child trying to make herself disappear.

The footsteps passed by, only a metre or two away, and then began to disappear towards the back of the crypt. Then the footsteps stopped. Ace waited, but there was no sound except the thumping of her own heart.

She looked at the Doctor, but she couldn't make out his expression in the dark. They waited for a minute, but heard nothing more. She felt the Doctor move beside her and peer round the corner. She followed him.

It was pitch black. The other oil lamp had disappeared. 'Where is it?' she whispered softly.

She heard the Doctor take out a box of matches and strike one. The match flared in the dark, and black shadows danced all around. The Doctor re-lit their oil lamp and held it up. The crypt was empty.

Ace didn't understand. 'Where is he?'

'Those noises you heard this morning.'

Suddenly Ace understood. 'A secret door!'

The Doctor had already put the lamp down on the ground and was pushing against parts of the wall.

'No, I think the noises were coming from over on this side.' Ace began pushing against the stones on the opposite wall. 'What do we do if we find something?' she asked, having no success.

She turned to try the wall at the far end of the crypt. Suddenly she stood too frightened to move. A small section of the far wall had swung silently open: Millington was standing behind it; his pistol pointed at Ace.

'I think this is what you were searching for, young lady.'

The Doctor turned quickly on hearing the familiar voice. He saw Millington's gun glinting in the shadows.

81

The commander stepped out into the crypt. 'Both of you, through here.'

Mr Wainwright stood in the pulpit and stared over the empty pews. He looked down at the book in his hands, and read.

When I was a child, I spake as a child, I understood as a child, I thought as a child: but when I became a man, I put away childish things.

He looked further down, and read some more:

And now remaineth faith, hope, love, these three; but the greatest of these is love.

What love? What hope? And, most of all, what faith? He couldn't feel any of these in his heart.

Steep metal steps led down a narrow passage behind the secret door of the crypt. A strange hissing sound came from the bottom.

Ace couldn't believe what she saw.

It was like a scene from some futuristic thriller. Technicians in protective rubber suits moved like aliens among laboratory equipment. Small jets of steam escaped from domed pressure vessels and lights blinked on control panels. At the far end of the room, a tunnel in one wall disappeared underground.

'Behold, Doctor: the end of the war. The end of all wars,' announced Millington from behind them. 'You were almost too late. We've finished here now. In twenty-four hours this cellar will be empty.'

The Doctor's face was dark. 'So that's what brought you here.'

He was looking at a small underground spring that was bubbling out of the wall, and trickling down into a ceramic vat beneath it. The water was slightly green in colour.

Ace still didn't understand. 'What is it? An underground stream?'

'A natural source of lethal poison, isn't it, commander? The Ultima project is just a cover. The Royal Navy is manufacturing chemical weapons. I imagine that underground tunnel leads all the way back to the naval camp.'

Millington's face twisted. 'You know, I can't make my mind up about you two. You've clearly convinced Dr Judson, yet we know absolutely nothing about you.'

'You're taking a bit of a risk, then, aren't you – showing us all this?'

'Not at all, Doctor. If I change my mind, I can always shoot you.'

'Ah, yes.'

'And I wanted to see how you would react. People sometimes get very irrational about chemical weapons. But once you're dead, what difference does it make what kind of weapon killed you?'

'I think the point is not those who die, but the effect on those who watch.'

'Very perceptive, Doctor. Dropping bombs to destroy an enemy city is only half of it. It must also terrify other enemy cities into surrender. The bombs must terrorize the enemy to its soul. And once the Nazis see what our planes are dropping on their cities . . .'

Ace could already see it. A black rain falling out of the night sky. 'But innocent people . . .'

'It will end the war, my dear. A few thousand will die. But hundreds of thousands will be saved. The war might continue for ten years, otherwise. Perhaps fifty years. Europe would be destroyed. These chemicals can save Europe, Doctor.'

'More horrible than the Well of Vergelmir.'

Millington suddenly froze, as though transfixed on a point. He slowly turned to the Doctor. 'What did you say?'

'The Well of Vergelmir. Deep beneath the ground, where broods of serpents spew their venom over the Great Ash Tree.'

'The Great Ash Tree,' whispered Millington. 'The soul of all the Earth.'

Ace was about to interrupt, but the Doctor raised his hand to silence her. The commander was staring into the Doctor's eyes. 'We have seen it, Doctor. You and I, we have seen hell. Come, I will show you everything.'

Millington turned back up the metal stairs.

'What's he on about?' whispered Ace.

'Old Norse mythology.' The Doctor smiled. 'I seem to have persuaded him that we're on his side.'

The Doctor and Ace hurried after Millington, back up into the church. Ace noticed Mr Wainwright sitting alone in one of the pews at the back of the church. 'Professor, what's wrong with the vicar?'

On hearing Ace's voice, Millington stopped dead, and turned to look at her. 'No girls,' he said to the Doctor. 'Leave her here.' He eyed Ace distastefully.

'What?' Ace strode towards the commander. 'You're beginning to aggravate me!'

The Doctor pulled her back. 'Ace, don't,' he whispered. 'He's mentally unbalanced. Don't argue with him. I'm sorry, you'll have to wait here.'

Ace's expression was sulky. But the Doctor didn't want to risk anything. 'Only for a short time. Give me an hour. Look, why don't you find out what's going on with Mr Wainwright?'

'All right – but you owe me one.'

84

The Doctor smiled, and turned back to Millington. 'Right – coming, commander.'

The Doctor hurried out after Millington. Ace wandered down the aisle to where Mr Wainwright was sitting. Her footsteps echoed round the church. She sat down by him. He was just staring silently up at the pulpit.

Ace wasn't sure what to say. 'Funny church this, isn't it?'

'I was just thinking . . .' Mr Wainwright continued to stare at the pulpit. 'Just remembering when I was a child. My father was vicar here then. He'd bring me here when no one else was about. It seemed such a warm place then, full of truth. Now it's just cold and empty.'

'Things always look different when you're small – more real.'

Mr Wainwright looked at Ace. She was startled to see that he'd been crying.

'But what's left to believe in when we're grown up? Every Sunday morning, I stand in the pulpit and I see all the faces looking up at me, waiting for me to give them something to believe in. What do I tell them?'

He seemed to be searching Ace's face for an answer. But she didn't have an answer. Vicars and priests were supposed to know all the answers. Why was he asking her? She looked back uncertainly. 'Don't you believe in anything?'

'I used to when I was younger. I used to believe there was good in the world – hope for the future.'

When I was a child, I spake as a child, I understood as a child, I thought as a child.

'Now: war, death, despair. What do I tell them?'

85

'You tell them there's good in the world and hope for the future.'

'But I don't believe it!'

'It doesn't matter! Just say it – live it – show them in everything you do.'

'But . . .'

'Believe me, I know what I'm talking about. Look, I had a sort of boyfriend once. He said he loved me. But whenever anyone else was around, he used to ignore me or joke about how stupid I was. And finally I realized that it doesn't matter whether someone says they love you, all that matters is what they show in their behaviour. So show these people you believe in the goodness of the world. That's all they want.'

'But what if it's not true?'

'Don't worry! The future's not so bad.'

Mr Wainwright looked at Ace. 'How can you know?'

She laughed. 'Have faith in me, vicar. I know these things.'

3

The Home Guard patrol walked along the pebbly shore, chatting and smiling as they defended Britain from the Nazi menace.

A little way ahead, Sorin, Trofimov and Vershinin lay crouched behind some rocks, watching the Home Guard men approach. Sorin glanced at the other two. Vershinin's young face glowed with anticipation, but Trofimov's was impassive. Sorin turned back and watched the Home Guard unit draw closer. He looked at Vershinin and nodded.

Vershinin tossed a small stone over the rock. It spun silently through the air and hit the cliff ten metres away. In a swift movement, the three commandos levered themselves over the rocks, and dropped down onto the confused Home Guard men like hawks hurtling out of an empty sky.

Three against six. It was quickly over. The commandos' knives flashed scarlet through the air, and five men were dead. One of the Home Guard was slightly faster; he backed away, his eyes like those of a terrified animal.

Trofimov grabbed the man from behind, slipped an arm round the man's neck and twisted sharply. There was a crack and the men fell to the ground.

Sorin looked round. 'Has anyone seen us?'

Vershinin smiled. 'It's as quiet as the grave.'

'Right, let's hide the bodies.' He looked at Trofimov, but the sergeant's face showed nothing.

Sergeant Leigh smiled, out of sight, on top of the cliff. He spoke into his radio. 'House guests returning to the honeymoon suite. Six toy soliders disabled. Repeat: all six toy soldiers disabled.'

He listened to the voice in his headset, and then replied. 'I confirm: house guests are secure. They haven't the slightest idea what's going on.' He smiled.

There was a noise from nearby. Leigh crawled through the long grass and found Miss Hardaker staring down at the commandos.

'What are you doing?' he hissed.

Miss Hardaker was startled to hear the voice so close to her. She turned and saw one of the marines from the naval camp crouching in the grass. 'Did you see that?' she stammered. 'We must inform the authorities.'

'We're informing no one,' interrupted Leigh. 'And

if you know what's good for you, you'll forget you ever saw anything.'

'But they're dead.'

Leigh's voice was hard. 'People die in war!' Then his face softened slightly. 'Now, you take my advice, Miss Hardaker: you go back home, have a nice cup of tea and forget everything. We'll take care of things.'

The Doctor followed Millington into the decryption room, where Dr Judson was muttering over the Ultima machine. Judson looked up at the commander and scowled.

'Where have you been, Millington? I need the central rotor unit unlocking.'

The Doctor stepped forward and admired the machine. 'So this is the Ultima machine?'

Judson swivelled round in his wheelchair. His eyes burned with fierce pride. 'Ah, yes. You haven't seen it yet, have you? This is a completely automatic computing machine. The most advanced in the world.'

The Doctor had to agree. There was no denying that the combination of creative genius and technical craftsmanship was superb. 'It's remarkable for the 1940s.'

Millington slowly smiled. 'This is just bait in the trap, Doctor.'

'A trap for the Germans?'

'The Russians.' His smile was that of a player who holds five aces.

The Doctor sensed something beginning to go wrong. 'But the Soviets are allies, even before the Americans.'

'Yes, of course, Doctor. But after the war, when they're no longer our allies . . .'

Millington turned the key and unlocked the central rotor unit. It slid out on frictionless bearings, six perfectly machined rotors that nested in an artifice of miniaturized wiring. 'This is what the Russians want, Doctor. The mind of the Ultima machine!'

The Doctor narrowed his eyes. This was where it began: the first step on the road of computer science. Microprocessors, analogue neuro-mimics, replicant intelligence. It all started with this simple work of mathematical ingenuity and engineering craftsmanship.

Dr Judson grabbed the Doctor's sleeve and whispered excitedly. 'Over thirty thousand combinations an hour with automatic negative thinking.'

The Doctor turned to Millington. 'And you're going to let the Russians steal it?'

'Orders from Whitehall. Look inside, Doctor. Look deep inside.'

The Doctor leaned forward to see inside the rotor unit. Almost invisible, buried deep beneath the chaos of wires, he saw a small glass flask. It seemed to glow with a faint green phosphorescence. The Doctor felt cold; he looked up.

Millington was no longer smiling. 'This way, Doctor.'

The Doctor followed the commander down to the far end of the camp towards one of the older stone buildings. It looked as though the camp had been built on the remains of a disused mine, and one or two of the old buildings had been left standing.

Inside, the Doctor looked round. He was gripped by an old feeling that he had hoped not to encounter again.

The building was vast, almost like a cathedral. The Doctor looked down the length of it and saw row upon row of black aircraft bombs that stood like tombstones and filled the great emptiness. Smaller weapons – mortars and grenades – were stacked high in crates. Each weapon carried a small yellow stencil: a skull and crossbones in which a gas-mask replaced the skull. Technicians in black rubber suits glided silently among the chemical weapons.

The far end of the building was filled with a green glow. It came from rows of huge glass jars that were filled with the deadly toxin.

Millington was standing in front of an air-tight chamber with glass windows. 'A demonstration, Doctor,' he called into the echoing vaults.

The Doctor walked slowly down a central aisle through the ranks of bombs. When he reached the commander, he saw that a cage of white doves had been placed inside the chamber and that the commander was operating two remote-control robot arms. A small loudspeaker outside the chamber hissed with the peaceful cooing of the doves inside.

Millington used one of the robot arms to pick up a small glass capsule inside the chamber. 'This small ampoule contains just a few drops of diluted toxin. It's mixed only one part in one thousand with a dispersion agent, and yet . . .'

Suddenly the Doctor knew what Millington was about to do. 'No, don't!'

But he was too late: Millington had cracked open the glass capsule. A small cloud of green vapour began to spread and fill the chamber. Over the loudspeaker, the cooing became agitated and then turned to loud squawks of agony. The Doctor could only imagine the suffering of the innocent doves as the green vapour scalded their lungs and burned like acid into their flesh.

Then the doves were silent.

Millington turned to the Doctor. 'Just think what a bombful could do to a city like Dresden or Moscow.'

The Doctor thought of it. Tens of thousands of innocent people screaming in terror as the acid gas dissolved away their flesh.

'It means the end of the war, Doctor. Two cities at most and the Nazis would surrender.'

The military mind was sickening. 'And Whitehall thinks the Soviets are so careless? Not only will they steal a booby-trapped computer, but they'll let you detonate it right inside the Kremlin?'

Millington smiled again. 'But that's the beauty of it, Doctor. The Soviets will detonate it themselves. They'll use the Ultima machine to decrypt our own ciphers. But Dr Judson has programmed it to self-destruct when it tries to decrypt a particular word. And when the political climate is appropriate, we shall include that word in one of our ciphers.'

'And the word is?'

'What else could it be, Doctor? Love.'

4

'You should have seen him! With his bare hands!' The commandos joined in Vershinin's smiles as he told them how Trofimov had killed the last, frightened Home Guard man. He slapped Trofimov heartily on the back. 'When it comes to killing, the sarge is an expert!'

But Trofimov didn't join in the celebration. As the others smiled excitedly together, he sat alone in a dark part of the cave. Sorin saw this, and he understood.

91

He stood over Trofimov and spoke quietly. 'I know how you feel. They were people's sons. They had wives, girlfriends, sisters – maybe even children. But these things have to be done, my friend.'

Trofimov looked up, and smiled in thanks. But it was an empty smile. Sorin shook Trofimov's shoulder warmly, and left the sergeant to his thoughts.

Sorin hadn't understood. *They had wives, girlfriends, sisters – maybe even children.* The words twisted in Trofimov's heart. A year ago, he wouldn't have given it a second thought. But a year ago, he didn't have a child of his own.

Miss Hardaker snatched the wet swimming costumes out of the girls' satchels. 'You will burn in the everlasting fires of hell!' she cried. 'You wicked, evil girls!'

Jean's face was insolent. 'Just because you've never been swimming.'

'You evil murderers!'

The word hit the two teenagers like a heavy blow. What did she mean?'

'They're dead! And you are responsible! If you hadn't disobeyed me, those poor Home Guards would never have gone looking for you. Now they lie dead on the sands. Dead! And you have killed them. You have black hearts. There's no love in heaven or earth for either of you. Nothing for you but pitiless damnation for the rest of your lives!'

The cellar beneath the crypt was almost empty now. The bombs were built, back at the naval camp, so this end of the operation had been closed down. All the valuable equipment had returned to the base the same way it had arrived – through the old mine tunnel –

and the last two technicians were now bricking up the entrance to the cellar from inside the tunnel.

One of the technicians was hammering large iron rods into the sides of the tunnel to provide more strength. Then they would pour liquid cement around the iron rods to seal off the tunnel.

He gave one of the rods a massive blow with a mallet, to drive it home, and heard the sound of falling bricks from inside the cellar. The two technicians instinctively ducked, expecting a cave-in, but the cellar was quiet again.

One of them took the oil lantern and peered through the narrow gap into the cellar.

Some of the old brickwork had collapsed round the edge of the tunnel entrance, but it was nothing that would hamper their work. Then he noticed something lying under the rubble. He reached out to pick it up and discovered it was some kind of old flask.

'Here, is this ours?' he called back to his colleague.

'Is it marked: government property?'

He peered at the old flask, but it didn't have any markings on it. 'Can't see anything.'

'Nothing to do with us, then. Leave it.'

He tossed the old flask on to a heap of rubbish they'd left behind, and returned to bricking up the entrance.

Millington glanced up at Captain Bates. 'Yes?'

'Thought you'd like to know, sir. They've finished closing-down operations in the church cellar.'

'Good.' Millington doodled aimlessly on a sheet of paper at his desk. 'Tell me, they didn't find anything unusual, did they?'

'Not to my knowledge, sir.'

Millington suddenly stared up at Bates. 'We can't

93

take any more risks. I want all radio transmitters and outside telephone lines disabled.'

'That might attract attention, sir,' warned Bates.

'Do it!' ordered Millington.

'Yes, sir!'

'And if there are any chess sets in the camp, I want them burned.'

'Chess sets?'

'Burned.'

'Yes, sir.'

Bates turned smartly, left the room and closed the door behind him.

Millington looked down at his random doodles. They seemed to have formed some kind of shape: the shape of an ancient flask.

Jean sat angrily on the edge of her bed. 'It wasn't our fault. We never asked for them to come looking for us.'

Phyllis had her knees drawn up under her chin, and was sniffling. 'I want to go home, Jean. I want to go back to London.'

Jean sat next to Phyllis, and put her arm round her. 'We can't, Philly. They think there might be more air raids.'

'I don't care. I want to go back to my mum and dad.'

'Come on, don't cry, Philly. It's this cottage that's making you feel that way. It's a witch's cottage. Come on, let's go back down to the sea. We can lie in the sun a bit longer.'

Trofimov was kneeling by a rock pool when he heard the girls' voices. He was washing his hands in the clean salt water. He was trying to wash the death off them and out of his soul, but it wouldn't go away.

'No, Jean, we mustn't,' he heard Phyllis calling.

'What do I care?' laughed Jean. 'We've nothing more to lose.'

Trofimov looked over the boulders. He saw the blonde girl run laughing into the sea. She was still wearing her light summer dress, which dragged in the water as it got wet.

'Come on, Philly! You're not going to be a baby doll, are you?'

'Well, just a paddle then.' And the brown-eyed girl who looked like Irena stepped carefully into the shallow waters.

The waves washed gently against Phyllis's legs.

'Come on! All the way in!' laughed Jean, aiming a large splash at Phyllis.

'Aagh!' laughed Phyllis, as the water drenched her face. 'You did that deliberately!'

'Come and catch me, then!'

Phyllis ran after Jean, kicking up water all around her. The tears and homesickness of half an hour ago dissolved in the sun-sparkled rain that drenched her. The two girls threw themselves into the water-fight like children. Finally, exhausted and laughing, Jean grabbed hold of Phyllis and pulled her down. They both tumbled beneath the surface.

Phyllis lay floating on her back. She could feel the folds of her summer dress drifting round her body and tugging gently at her. It was so warm in the water. So warm and peaceful.

'Here, Philly. Look at that.'

Phyllis went on floating. 'What is it?'

'It looks like some kind of mist, coming towards us.'

95

'Who cares? It's warm in the water.'

'Yeah.' But Jean's voice was anxious.

Phyllis felt the first wisps of the mist drift across her face. They were chilly.

Jean's voice was more concerned. 'Philly, I can't see you.'

Without thinking, Trofimov stood up. The sea fog had completely enveloped the two English girls and their voices had disappeared. There wasn't even any sound of splashing. Just a cold silence.

As quickly as it had filled the bay, the fog drifted away again. The sun shone weakly in the sky. Trofimov looked across the smooth water's surface. The two girls had disappeared.

He looked around, expecting to see them catching their breath further along the shore, but they were nowhere to be seen. He emerged from behind the boulders and strode towards the sea.

The air was still, but his mind struggled chaotically. Irena! He must save Irena! She was drowning! But where was she?

He looked around wildly, but saw nothing except a high bank of fog looming ahead and drawing closer. The cold fog quickly engulfed him, but he waded into the water. He must find Irena! Tnen he heard her voice.

He peered into the fog and saw two figures – two girls splashing in the water and laughing. He thought that one of them was Irena. But when she turned to look at him, he knew he was wrong. Both girls had ghastly white faces with rich, ruby-red lips.

'Look,' said Phyllis, smiling.

'Oh yes, a man,' Jean laughed with a slightly girlish voice that made Trofimov shiver. Then she called to him. 'Are you looking for us? Are you watching us?'

Her languid voice caressed his mind with the hand of a mistress. 'He's watching us, you know,' she smiled to Phyllis.

Phyllis lifted an arm to beckon Trofimov. 'If you want to watch, you've got to come in the water with us.'

'Yes, you've got to come in the water.'

The two voices seemed to overload his senses, drawing him forwards. The rich ruby lips that seemed to touch his own; the sweet, sweet taste of blood; and the deep musk scent of the darkness in girls.

'Come on,' urged Phyllis, 'it's nice in the water. You'll like it. Nice and warm.'

'Blood warm,' coaxed Jean.

Trofimov had no will of his own. The liquid voices drew him deeper into the water.

'He's coming, coming into the water.'

'Nobody's forcing him. Nobody ever forces you to go into the water.'

'But everybody wants to. Deep down, everybody wants to go into the water.'

'Come on. Come and play with us.'

The two voices turned into a cruel laugh. Trofimov looked round, but it was too late. An inhuman hand burst from the water and grabbed at the Russian. Then another hand, and another. The scalpel-edged fingernails slashed through his tunic and into his flesh. Trofimov struggled in terror as a dozen inhuman hands dragged him down into the water.

Soon the water was still. Quite still – and blood red.

97

A Victorian Storyteller

A letter from Abraham Stoker to his wife, Florence:

Whitby
May 23rd, 18–

My dearest wife,

I was delighted to receive your telegram this morning, and I await your arrival here with eager
anticipation.

Sir Henry and I travelled to Scarborough yesterday, with a view to attending a performance by Mr
Grossmith at the Spa Theatre; and a curious circum-
stance occurred during our journey. We decided to
break the journey at a small village situated no more
than a mile from M– bay, a scenic attraction of
mysterious beauty, and we sought out an inn where
we may take luncheon. The innkeeper was naturally
most delighted to receive a guest of Sir Henry's
celebrity and stature: and he fell into conversation
with us. He happened to mention the most tragic
death of a local girl, not three days ago, so (out of
natural curiosity) I pressed him for further details. It
appears that the girl, who was of some nineteen years,

and formerly a virtuous daughter, had become some-thing of a wayward creature, and had taken to visiting the bay with lewd men. Naturally, this became the subject of local gossip (much to the grief of her Christian parents), which held that the girl was bound to come to no good from her activities. Then, three evenings past, she had failed to return home for the night, and her parents became greatly alarmed. The next morning, a search was mounted, and the girl's dead body was discovered near the cliff-top. Upon inspection, she was revealed to bear several cuts about the throat and neck, and the local doctor pronounced her to be completely drained of blood; but the curios-ity was that there was no blood on the ground nearby. The magistrate offered the opinion that she had been murdered elsewhere (for who knows what reason?), and that the body had subsequently been brought to the place where it was discovered; hence, the absence of blood on the ground where she lay. But some of the villagers were still unconvinced by this explanation (according to our host). These superstitious folk believe the unfortunate girl to be the latest victim of unnatural creatures who are reputed to live in the waters off M– bay. Local legend would have it that these creatures devour the blood of humans, and that they are afflicted with eternal life. (To think, my dear wife, that we have vampires living in our own islands!)

Naturally, the whole episode was buzzing in my mind for the rest of the day; and, even now, the story will not leave me in peace. I begin to believe that the seeds of some greater story may lie in this tragic incident. Perhaps I shall know better when you arrive.

Your beloved husband,
Bram

Chronicle IV

Vampire City!

1

The Doctor stared at the bonfire of burning chess sets as he strode past it. Things were happening too quickly. He hurried into the hut where the Wrens had their quarters.

A couple of young women were playing cards quietly; a third one lay on her bunk reading a magazine. Joe Loss and his band played softly on the wireless. Kathleen was just rocking Audrey to sleep in a cot half-hidden beside her own bunk.

The Doctor's head appeared round the door, and he peered inside. He saw Kathleen, and smiled. 'Hallo. You haven't seen Ace, have you? I was expecting her to meet me back here.'

Kathleen smiled warmly. 'I'm sorry, I haven't. But I'll keep my eyes open for her.'

The Doctor looked down at Audrey who was gurgling happily to herself. 'What are you going to do with her?'

'Oh, something'll turn up.' Kathleen looked hopefully at the Doctor in case he might suggest some solution. 'One of the girls said she'd ask her sister if Audrey could stay for a few days, just until I sort something out.'

But she knew in her heart that the sister would say no. She looked down at the happy little bundle who had no idea of the trouble she was causing. How could anyone take against a sweet little thing like this?

Kathleen looked back at the Doctor, and noticed he was smiling too. 'Do you have any family yourself?' she asked.

The Doctor looked up, a little sadly. 'I don't know,' he sighed.

'I'm sorry. It's the war, isn't it? It must be terrible not knowing.'

'Yes,' said the Doctor. How right she was. Were there others like him, he wondered, in a distant galaxy somewhere? Would he ever know? (*Ever* is a terribly long time.)

He stood up quickly and banished such thoughts from his mind. 'Can't stay. Must look for Ace.'

He hurried across the compound towards the decryption room. Dr Judson was hunched over the teletype unit. New Viking letters had been stuck over the ordinary keyboard alphabet, and Dr Judson was typing the final inscription into the machine.

Nurse Crane sat indifferently to one side.

The Doctor breezed in. 'You haven't seen my assistant, have you? I'm getting quite worried.'

'Quiet!' interrupted Dr Judson. Then he sat back and smiled. 'Now then. Let's see what lies encrypted in these carvings, shall we?'

He flicked a switch, and the machine chattered into life. The relays clicked rapidly and the rotor wheels whirred. Judson watched in excitement.

The Doctor leaned forward anxiously and watched.

101

Suddenly, the machine stopped. There was a moment's silence before the teleprinter started to clatter. Even Nurse Crane seemed interested, as the machine began printing its message: LET . . . THE . . . CHAINS . . . OF . . . FENRIC . . . SHATTER.

The Doctor gave a slight sigh of relief.

Judson sat back triumphantly. 'You see! A thinking machine! Even with an alphabet more than a thousand years old, the Ultima machine can reveal its meaning.'

The Doctor smiled. 'Well, it can translate it, at least. Who knows what it might mean?'

'What?'

'It can print out a translation in English. But what does it mean?'

'How should I know? Some stuff and nonsense to do with all that Viking mythology, I shouldn't wonder. Better ask Millington if you want explanations. Come on, Crane. Back to the office.'

Nurse Crane expertly wheeled Dr Judson out of the decryption room and back into his office. The Doctor followed.

'You've known Commander Millington for quite some time, then?' the Doctor asked.

'Oh yes, I've known Millington since before . . . since before my accident.'

The door flew open and in wandered Ace. 'Hi, everybody.'

'Ah, you're back.' The Doctor stood and turned to Ace. 'I need to have a word with your two young friends.'

'Jean and Phyllis? They'll be with the old dragon.'

'Good. Back in a mo. I'm just going to requisition some transport.'

'Great! Bags I drive!'

The Doctor frowned and disappeared.

The office was quiet except for the rapid tap of Dr Judson's chalk on the blackboard as he scribbled down more equations. Nurse Crane was glaring at Ace, so Ace smiled at her: she looked away.

Ace watched Dr Judson. She noticed that he'd chalked a copy of the final Viking inscription on one blackboard, a series of regular lines and angles chalked in neat rows and columns. On the other board, she saw a flow chart representing the flip-flop game she had borrowed earlier. She pulled the game from her duffle bag, and looked at it. The pattern of coloured windows illustrated the mechanism inside: an array of simple logic gateways. If the window is blue, then the marble falls to the right. If the window is yellow, then the marble falls to the left. The simplest of logic machines. She dropped a marble in one of the holes at the top and watched it clatter down through the flip-flops.

'Shut up,' snapped Dr Judson.

But Ace wasn't listening. She was looking at the blackboards. The regular lines and angles of the Viking inscriptions next to the lines and angles of the flip-flop logic gates. She dropped another marble through the flip-flop game.

'I said shut up!'

'I know what it is,' Ace murmured quietly, for fear that if she spoke too loud she might disturb something in the universe and her sudden realization would crumble.

Dr Judson threw down his chalk and angrily turned on her. 'I'm trying to work!'

'The Viking inscription. I know what it is.'

'Yes, it means: let the chains of Fenric shatter. I

already know that. Now can we have some quiet, please?'

Ace's eyes shone with excitement. 'No, look. It's a logic diagram.'

Dr Judson's irritation instantly disappeared. 'What?'

Ace pointed at the chalk lines. 'Look. This is a logic diagram you've drawn for the flip-flop thingy. And these inscriptions are a logic diagram for something else! Don't you see?'

Indeed Dr Judson did see – his face was blank with amazement. 'But it's so complex for a game.'

Ace smiled. 'That's because it's not meant for a game. It's for a computer.'

Dr Judson was unable to move for a moment while his mind tried to grasp the vast potential of the girl's words. Then he was galvanized into action. He frantically tried to propel his wheelchair out of the office. 'Crane! Take me to the decryption room!'

Ace watched as Nurse Crane hurried after Dr Judson, then Ace sauntered out to catch up with the Doctor. She was pleased with herself.

'And the half-time score: Perivale, six hundred million; rest of the universe, nil.'

2

Miss Hardaker carefully placed the record on the turntable. She wound the handle until the spring inside was tight and released the lever. The record began to spin. She swung the gramophone arm over and placed the needle at the start of the record.

The dark opening chords of Fauré's Requiem filled

the living room of the cottage. Miss Hardaker went and sat in her armchair and listened as the choir intoned the opening lines.

Requiem æternam dona eis Domine.

Eternal rest grant them, O Lord.

Unwillingly, her mind drifted back – back to Maidens' Point, back to when she was only nineteen. The shame of it. Only nineteen and with child – and she was unmarried. The looks, the whispers, the silences. A mother's pitying glances, and a father who never spoke another word to her until the day he died.

The infant itself died before it reached the age of two, but the stigma never died. Folk never forget. No matter how upright she lived the rest of her days, she would always remain an outcast from the village. Her life was forever besmirched.

A sound in the doorway interrupted the spinster's bitter thoughts. She turned to see Jean and Phyllis staring at her. Their eyes were dark and sunken, in ghastly pale faces, and their lips were swollen and red.

The two girls walked slowly towards Miss Hardaker. They raised their hands as they approached, and she saw their fingernails glitter like knife-blades.

'No,' she ordered, but the girls continued to advance. They smiled a little as they saw fear fill their victim.

'No,' moaned Miss Hardaker, 'no, I beg you.'

But the girls drew their nails slowly across her skin, and slowly the life trickled out of her.

The dark voices on the gramophone observed it all.

Kyrie eleison. Christe eleison.

Lord, have mercy. Christ, have mercy.

* * *

'This is it, Judson!' Millington grabbed Dr Judson's shoulder.

'A little respect for the wheelchair please, sir,' admonished Nurse Crane. 'He's an invalid.'

'I'm not an invalid – I'm a cripple! And I'm also a genius! Now, shut up, both of you!' Dr Judson returned to his work of altering the Ultima machine's wiring to match the logic diagram in the inscription.

'All we need now is the flask.' Millington's eyes were filled with madness. 'The machine can unlock its secrets.'

The Doctor and Ace crept cautiously through the open door of Miss Hardaker's cottage. The Doctor looked round. 'Hallo. Anybody home?'

Silence, apart from the regular click of the gramophone needle sitting at the middle of the slowly revolving record. The Doctor lifted the arm, and switched off the motor.

'Professor.'

The Doctor turned to look.

Miss Hardaker's body was sitting upright in her armchair. Her eyes seemed to be staring dead ahead and her mouth was open in a silent scream. Deep, bloodless cuts slashed through the veins of her neck and her skin was white.

'Just like the one at Maidens' Point,' the Doctor grimly observed. 'Completely drained of blood.'

He drew his hand over the eyes, and closed them. May she rest in peace.

'The question is: where are your two friends?'

The mist drifted among the graves in the churchyard; Jean and Phyllis seemed to drift with it. They stopped a few metres behind Mr Wainwright, but he knew they were there, even without seeing them.

He clutched his Bible, to give him strength. 'I know who you are.'

Phyllis's face was empty. 'You've always known us, Wainwright.'

Full of fear, Mr Wainwright forced himself to turn and face the two creatures. The only traces of humanity left in their faces were cruelty and evil. He could barely believe the transformation could be so rapid. Proof that the old tales were indeed true. 'But vampires are just superstition. Why?'

Jean took a step forwards. 'We have black hearts. Our souls were lost on the day we were born.'

'That's not true! No one is lost.'

Phyllis stared at him. 'Everyone is lost, Wainwright.'

The two creatures stepped towards him. He quickly held up the Bible to ward them off. 'No further! This is holy. It will destroy you.'

Jean smiled cruelly. 'Objects don't harm us. It's human belief that hurts us. And you stopped believing when the bombs started falling.'

'That's not true. I'm not frightened of German bombs.'

'Not German bombs.' Phyllis's voice sought out the truth. 'British bombs.'

'British bombs falling on German cities,' insisted Jean. 'Killing innocent German children.'

'No!' The Bible fell from his hands in grief as he realized the creatures were right. There was nothing he could believe in any longer. The Nazis were evil, he knew that. And the British were supposed to be fighting for good. But how could they be good if they slaughtered innocent people? How could there be any good at all in the world?

107

The two creatures smiled, and advanced on the broken Mr Wainwright.

'NO!' cried the Doctor. His shout echoed through the churchyard. Jean and Phyllis halted; the Doctor and Ace ran in front of Mr Wainwright.

Ace looked at the two creatures in horror. 'What's happened to you? What are you doing?'

Phyllis looked back at Ace. The eyes that were once warm and brown were now empty and dead. 'You should have come in the water with us, then we'd be together.'

'GO!' shouted the Doctor in a terrible cry. 'Go now!' He stared at the two creatures with an expression so dark and powerful that it seemed almost evil.

The two creatures began to back away into the mists. But Jean's eyes were fixed on Mr Wainwright. 'We go. But we'll return for you, Wainwright.'

The mists enveloped the two creatures. The Doctor turned to Mr Wainwright. 'Are you all right?'

Mr Wainwright was shaken, but he pulled himself together. 'We must tell Commander Millington, Doctor. We must warn them.'

'That's exactly what we won't do! They'll just start shooting anything and everything. No, as long as Dr Judson doesn't find out what the final inscription really is, they're out of harm's way. And he's a typical blinkered scientist.'

'Hell.'

Ace's interruption stopped the Doctor dead. As soon as he saw her face, he knew what she'd done.

'You should have warned me,' she protested.

'Come on! We've got to stop him!' The Doctor broke into a run and made across the churchyard in the direction of the naval camp.

* * *

108

Dr Judson slid the central rotor unit back into position and connected up the leads. 'Now then, Millington. Let's see, shall we?'

'Yes, quick!'

Judson turned to the keyboard, and began to type: LET THE CHAINS OF FENRIC SHATTER. The relays began to click and the rotors whirred into action, obeying their instructions from more than a thousand years ago. It was as though some superbeing had breathed life into the machine.

The teleprinter suddenly started to chatter out a stream of words: WULFAGA . . . OTTAR . . . HORIK . . . ESTRID . . . SIGVALD . . . HAKON . . . FRIDREK . . . WULFSTAN . . . EADRIC . . . EMMA . . . The machine went on printing.

Millington stared at them. 'They're Viking names. What do they mean, Judson?'

'I don't know!'

'You built the damned machine!'

'It's running at four times maximum speed! It's impossible!'

After more than a thousand years in the sea, the creatures began to rise. Their abominable forms broke the surface and they started to stride ashore. An army rose from the sea.

Their bodies were horrifying mutations of the humans they had once been. Their skin was slimy and slightly wrinkled, like huge white slugs with legs and arms. Their eyes were swollen and bulbous, closed like a foetus in its uterus. And their mouths had turned into large suckers for draining blood.

Some of them still had traces of human origins – vestigial ears, or a skeleton that was vaguely humanoid – and these creatures still had scraps of recent human clothing hanging off them. But those that had been waiting for a century or more were now completely changed. Instead of clothing, they had thin strands of glistening filament that hung about their bodies. Among the filaments and linked with them were old metal objects – objects that had either been discarded in the waters down the centuries or taken from the creatures' victims. Keys, locks, coins, scissor-blades were now welded by an iridescent coral into a kind of chain mail.

A faint screeching sound filled the air, like bats in a cave. An audible backwash of the creatures' telepathic calls.

Seek out the fluid of life.

The Doctor and Ace burst into the decryption room, followed by Mr Wainwright.

'Stop the machine!' cried the Doctor.

Millington spun round. 'Get out of here!'

'You must stop that machine!'

'You take your orders from me, Judson!'

The Doctor looked round frantically. He saw a power cable running from the electricity supply box to the Ultima machine. 'Ace, the cable!'

Ace grabbed the cable and ripped it out of the machine. All the control lights on the machine died, but the rotors and relays continued to chatter away at breakneck speed. The teleprinter paper strip continued to list unknown names. The machine was running without power! The Doctor looked at it in horror.

'You're too late, Doctor!' laughed Millington.

Bates burst through the open door. Millington turned to him. 'Captain, no one is to touch the Ultima machine. It must complete its task.'

110

'Yes, sir!'

The Doctor turned to Millington. 'There's just one problem, commander. You've weakened the camp's defences precisely so that some Soviet commandos can steal the machine.'

Millington's expression turned to horror as he realized the Doctor was right. 'Captain, radio for reinforcements!'

'But sir, you ordered that all radio transmitters be disabled. I've set Perkins on to it.'

'What!'

Perkins was delivering a final axe-blow to the last radio transmitter when his commanding officer burst in, followed by the base commander and a few other people.

Millington stared at the wrecked radio equipment. Perkins had smashed it all.

Perkins stood to attention, the axe in his hand. 'Sir! Radio transmitters disabled, as ordered, sir!' he barked.

The Doctor stepped forward. 'Splendid job, Perkins! Excellent work!'

Perkins smiled proudly.

The Doctor smiled back. 'Now put it all back together again.'

The Doctor wheeled round, and marched out.

3

The Doctor paced broodily about the bunk room.

'We don't have long,' he muttered. 'A few hours at most.'

Ace was anxious. 'But what's happened to Jean and Phyllis?'

Mr Wainwright looked up. 'Dark legends. In the story of Dracula, this is where he came ashore, leaped from a wrecked boat in the form of a huge wolf.'

Ace's eyes grew large in amazement. 'You mean Jean and Phyllis are vampires?'

'They're not called vampires,' interrupted the Doctor irritably. 'They're called haemovores – *Homo haemovorax*. This is what *Homo sapiens* evolves into, thousands of years in the future as the Earth is dying. Creatures with an insatiable hunger for blood. That's why they're living in the sea at Maidens' Point. Clean salt water has similar properties to human blood plasma.'

This time it was Mr Wainwright's turn to look amazed. 'The future? I don't understand. How can you know about the future?'

The Doctor's face was sad. 'Because I've seen it,' he sighed, remembering the chemical-rotted land-scapes of a once-beautiful green planet. He shook the barren scenes from his mind and turned to Mr Wainwright. 'How good are your parish records?'

'They go back to the eighteenth century. Why?'

'Because I think it's time for a spot of local history.' Then the Doctor noticed that Ace was looking upset. 'What's the matter?' he asked gently.

'I was just thinking . . .' Ace's face was full of concern. 'What if the vampires – I mean haemovores – what if they get into the camp? The little baby . . . Kathleen.'

The Doctor thought back to the bouncy, argumentative teenage waitress he'd first met in the Refreshment Bar on Iceworld. And now here she was, almost a different person – a young woman. 'Once upon a time, you'd have dropped everything to do something exciting.'

'Yeah, I know, but I just want to make sure they're all right.'

The Doctor smiled. 'Catch us up. We'll be at the church.'

Ace gave the Doctor a quick hug. 'Thanks,' and hurried off to Kathleen's hut.

She'll be leaving me soon, the Doctor thought sadly. He turned to Mr Wainwright. 'Well, shall we go?'

Mr Wainwright's expression was troubled. 'Those two vampire girls – they said they'd return for me.'

The Doctor understood the young vicar's fears. 'You can stay here, if you prefer.'

Mr Wainwright looked up at the Doctor. 'No, Doctor, I can't,' he said. 'I can't run away from it. I must face them again.'

Kathleen was packing her clothes and belongings into a suitcase when Ace looked into the Wrens' quarters. Ace understood what was happening. There was no one who could look after little Audrey, so Kathleen had been forced to leave. It's a bad life for lonely mothers.

Ace tried to sound cheerful. 'Hi. How's the little horror?'

Kathleen indicated Audrey's basket lying on one of the bunks. 'Sleeping. I've just fed her.'

'You should have told me; I'd have come and helped. Let me know next time.'

'All right,' smiled Kathleen.

Ace went to look at the sleeping baby. Audrey was breathing peacefully, dreaming of whatever babies dream of. She smelled warm and sweet, and Ace couldn't imagine anyone who would want to harm such a gentle little thing.

Kathleen folded some baby clothes and laid them alongside a chess set which she had saved from Perkins' bonfire. Ace went to stand beside her. 'Where will you go?'

Kathleen smiled. 'Oh, don't worry about me. I'll manage. Frank's got shore leave in a few weeks.'

'Who's Frank? Your boyfriend?'

Kathleen looked up, surprised. 'No, he's my husband.'

Ace suddenly noticed that Kathleen was wearing a wedding ring. 'Oh, sorry, I didn't know you were married.'

'I've got a baby.'

'Yeah, I know,' Ace tried to explain. 'I just thought, you know . . .'

'Well, you can stop thinking it.'

It was clear that Ace had offended Kathleen. In Ace's Perivale, she'd known lots of women with babies and who weren't married, and no one thought anything of it. But things were different in 1943. Ace tried to put things right. 'No, I didn't mean that. I just didn't know.'

Kathleen saw in Ace's face that she hadn't meant any harm, so she relaxed and smiled. 'It's OK.'

Ace looked at a photo of a man in a naval uniform, which Kathleen had placed carefully in the suitcase. 'Where is he?' asked Ace.

'Merchant Navy.' Kathleen looked proudly at the photo of her Frank. 'On the Atlantic convoys.'

Ace was thoughtful. 'I used to think that I'm never going to get married. But I'm not so sure now. There's a lot of things I'm not sure about now. Everything seems to be changing.'

'It's the war.'

'Yeah.' Ace turned to Kathleen. 'Look, take care, won't you?'

'Thanks. You too.'

'No, I mean really take care. There's bad things going on here. Get away from this place. Take Audrey and get as far away as possible.'

Sorin knelt by Trofimov's dead body on the shore.

Vershinin crouched beside him. 'I'm sorry, sir. I know you and the sarge had been together a long time.'

Sorin said nothing, but reached into Trofimov's pocket and took out a small pocketbook. Inside, there was a photograph. It was a portrait of Trofimov, his wife Irena and their ten-month-old daughter, just two of the thousands of nameless widows and orphans left to fend for themselves after the war. But Trofimov hadn't been killed by the war.

'Captain!' shouted Vershinin suddenly.

Sorin looked up to see a black mist rolling in off the sea. And advancing out of the fog, towards the commandos, he saw hideous figures with swollen eyes and mouths. Phyllis and Jean were among them, their bloated red lips now looking less and less human. A faint screeching sound seemed to fill the air all around.

The commandos raised their rifles to fire.

'Save your bullets,' called Sorin. 'Everyone pull back.'

'Captain . . .' argued Vershinin.

'I said pull back,' ordered Sorin crisply. 'And don't turn away from them, or you're dead.'

The commandos quickly pulled back inland. The haemovores followed, leaving a slimy trail behind them. The screeching sound was everywhere.

'Over there!' shouted Sorin, indicating a barren patch of land to one side.

The commandos regrouped where ordered and prepared for the creatures to attack. But the haemovores took no notice of the commandos. They seemed to be heading towards the village.

Vershinin watched them pass. He held his Tokarev ready. 'What are they?'

'Six months ago,' explained Sorin, 'a small Red Army sabotage team was sent into German-occupied Romania – Transylvania region. They disappeared. Sergeant Trofimov and I took a rescue team, but we found only one survivor. He was just like Gayev, his mind in pieces. He kept talking about dead men walking out of the black fog. In my report, I said he'd been listening to too much local gossip about vampires.'

'Vampires? But they don't exist.'

'Of course they don't.' Sorin narrowed his eyes and looked at Vershinin. 'But if you want to see the sun rise tomorrow, you'd better start sharpening some wooden stakes. Bullets are useless.'

Vershinin looked back to the hellish creatures that were still just visible in the gloomy fog.

But Sorin was troubled by something else. Why had he and Trofimov been chosen for this mission? Had someone selected them specially, because they had been to Transylvania?

'Vershinin, you stay here. You two come with me. I want to know what those creatures are looking for.'

'Millington, we're wasting our time on some superstition!'

Dr Judson pounded his fist on the desk in exasperation. The Ultima machine was running out of control,

116

and all Millington could do was sit in his office drawing doodles of antique bottles!

But Millington was calm.

'The Viking legends will come true, Judson. The treasure will be brought to us. And with it, all the dark powers of Fenric shall be ours.'

'Yes, yes, I know – let the chains of Fenric shatter. But what of my chains?' Judson banged angrily at his wheelchair.

A haunted look suddenly filled Millington's eyes, and he looked up. 'That was more than twenty years ago. Why must you remind me? I offer you everything.'

Ace caught up with the Doctor and Mr Wainwright just as they reached the church.

'Why does your bell tower look like a fortress?' she asked the young vicar as they went into the vestry. 'It's as if the people who built it were expecting trouble.'

'I'm pretty certain there's no record of any battles taking place here.'

'Today's entry has still to be written,' warned the Doctor, and he handed two large volumes of parish records to Mr Wainwright. 'Now then, you're looking for anyone who seems to have had Viking ancestors. The surnames will probably give you a clue. About two hundred years ago. Ace, you come with me, down to the crypt.'

In the cellar beneath the crypt, a pulsating green light radiated from the mysterious flask and cast ghastly shadows across the derelict laboratory equipment. As the yellow glow of an oil lantern approached from the crypt, the green light began to fade and die. By the time the Doctor and Ace entered the cellar, the old flask was lying dull and lifeless among the equipment.

'So what are we looking for?' asked Ace.

'The Viking inscriptions said they were carrying treasure from the Orient.'

'I've been there.'

'Where?'

'Leyton Orient. Second-round cup match. We slaughtered them three-nil.'

'Just look for something evil!' exclaimed the Doctor in exasperation. Really, what on earth had Ace been doing during geography lessons!

Ace started poking through the equipment. There was some useful stuff here that might come in handy when she next had a chance to sit down and do some chemistry experiments: some clean test tubes and stoppers, rubber tubes, pipettes, and a really neat pestle and mortar. She started stuffing them in her duffle bag. There was also an old flask that looked like junk, but Ace reckoned that it might be worth a bob or two if she cleaned it up.

'Doctor! Doctor!' Mr Wainwright's voice called excitedly down from the vestry.

The Doctor hurried up the stairs into the crypt to find out what the commotion was about. Ace shoved the old flask in her bag and ran after him.

In the vestry, Mr Wainwright was quite beside himself with excitement.

'Look, Doctor! I've found it!' he exclaimed. 'Exactly as you said!'

'What is it, vicar?' Ace was dying to know what he'd discovered.

Mr Wainwright was pointing at a page in one of the record books. 'Look, here are your Vikings, or

118

descendants of them at any rate. Look: Joseph Sund-vik, and wife Florence. Daughters: Sarah, Martha, Jane, Clara, Annie.'

'The curse of Fenric,' murmured the Doctor. 'Passed down through the generations.'

HANNAH . . . JOSEPH . . . SARAH . . . MARTHA . . . JANE . . . CLARA . . . ANNIE . . . MARY . . . WILLIAM . . .

The Ultima machine continued to chatter out its meaningless names.

'A fine piece of detective work, Mr Wainwright. Now see if you can find out which daughters got married. I need to know their surnames after they married.'

'I'll see what I can do.'

'Here, Professor?' Ace tried to attract the Doctor's attention.

'What is it?'

'Where's this water coming from?' Ace was pointing at a pool of water in the middle of the floor.

'Oh, it'll be the skylight,' explained Mr Wain-wright. 'It always leaks when it's raining.'

Another splash hit the ground. The Doctor's face was grim. 'Except it isn't raining.'

They looked up to the skylight above them just in time to see the window smash. Shards of glass show-ered down on them, and revealed behind the skylight window the hideous faces of two haemovores.

Ace leapt backwards to avoid the falling glass, and as she did so, two inhuman arms crashed through the window behind her and grabbed at her shoulder. She twisted to free herself from the clawing hands and their flashing nails.

The Doctor snatched up a candlestick and started

attacking the arms that were clutching Ace. She managed to break herself free and looked quickly round for another weapon to help the Doctor.

'The door!' shouted the Doctor. 'Lock the door!'

Ace spun round. She saw that the door was beginning to open and hurled herself at it in an attempt to close it. Several haemovore hands, however, had pushed through the gap and clawed at her. Mr Wainwright grabbed the second candlestick and started swinging it at the creatures' hands.

With a final heave, Ace managed to shut the door and slide the bolt home. Mr Wainwright went to join the Doctor fighting at the window.

'Vampire city!' gasped Ace. 'Stay here. I'll go and fetch help!'

She disappeared through the door up to the bell-tower, just as the Doctor and Mr Wainwright managed to beat off the haemovores that were attacking through the window.

The Doctor looked round breathlessly. 'Where's Ace?' he demanded.

'Bell-tower.'

'No! We've got to stop her!'

The Doctor rushed to the door leading up the bell-tower, but as he reached the porch, he was confronted by several more haemovores.

'Back here!' shouted Mr Wainwright, dragging the Doctor back into the vestry and slamming the door shut.

'No!' cried the Doctor in anguish. 'We've got to help her!'

But it was too late. The Doctor and Mr Wainwright were trapped inside the vestry.

Ace was on her own.

* * *

120

Ace clambered quickly up the spiral stone stairs of the bell-tower. She was beginning to get dizzy from twisting round and round, but she could hear the screeching of the haemovores following her and knew that she couldn't stop.

She reached a narrow window in the wall. A short, rusty spike was nailed into the stones beneath it. This could have to do!

She pulled one of her rock-climbing ropes from her duffle bag. There wasn't time to bother with clips and pulleys, so she just knotted it several times to the spike. Then she took a step back, and kicked at the glass window. The old panes of glass shattered. Ace kicked them all out before throwing the rope through the window. She made sure there were no sharp edges of glass left in the frame, and then began to climb backwards through the window.

She heard the screeching in the bell-tower as she steadied herself, hanging on the rope outside. She kicked about with her feet to try to catch the loose end beneath her. Finally she managed to grip it between her feet. Ace slowly began to work her way down the rope to the church roof beneath her. From there she could drop another rope down the outside of the church and run to the village for help.

But as she neared the bottom of the rope, she felt sharp fingernails cutting at her legs. She looked down, and saw the church roof covered in haemovores, which crawled there like leeches. Their hands grabbed at her legs, trying to pull her down.

In the graveyard, Sorin looked up at the haemo-vores that crawled over the church roof. He saw the British woman he had released, struggling to free herself from the creatures.

'Come on!' he shouted to the two commandos with him, as he raced towards the church.

Ace managed to pull herself free from the clutches of the haemovores beneath her, and she started to drag herself back up the outside of the bell-tower. She looked up for way of some escape, but more haemovores were crawling through the window above her. Somehow they were able to cling to the outside wall; they began to crawl down towards her. Ace desperately looked round for some way out – some window she could crawl through – but there was nothing.

The haemovores' hands pulled her down and dragged her back down towards the church roof. There was nothing she could do to resist. She struggled, but the arms were all around her, clutching at her and pulling at her head. They pulled her head back and forced her neck forwards – her neck was exposed to the horrible, swollen mouths that drew closer and closer.

'Look out, Doctor!'

The door to the vestry was beginning to splinter.

The Doctor and Mr Wainwright rushed to hold it up and keep the haemovores out. Already, razor-hard nails were slashing through the soft wood.

'Hold them for five seconds!' shouted the Doctor.

'I'm not sure I can!'

'You must! Have faith in yourself! You must have faith!'

Mr Wainwright heaved against the door with all his strength; the Doctor stood back in the centre of the room. He put his fingers to his temples and closed his eyes.

'Faith,' he murmured to himself. 'Faith in . . .' His mind went blank.

It was no good! He couldn't think of anything. What did he have faith in? He had to think of something quickly. He had faith in goodness, of course, but it had to be something solid, something he could concentrate on.

Mr Wainwright was struggling against the haemovores on the other side of the door, but there were too many of them and his strength was dying.

The Doctor tried to think. Faith in what? No, not what, but who! That's it! Faith in whom? Yes, Susan, his granddaughter. Concentrate on that! Concentrate on Susan, and on Ian and Barbara. Yes, he always had faith in them – his companions during his travels. Susan, Ian, Barbara, Vicki, Stephen . . .

As the Doctor's concentration grew deeper, there seemed to be a sound, far away. Beyond the screeching of the haemovores, the pure, beautiful sound of voices, like the songs of angels echoing through space. Songs summoned from the very edges of time, drawing closer, carried on wings across deserts of eternity. A sound to touch the heart of every living thing, a sound pure and true. Suddenly the sound filled the room – a golden chorus that shimmered all around. The psychic sound of pure faith.

Except, Mr Wainwright seemed not to hear it. He just continued struggling against the door.

Only the Doctor heard the radiant sound.

And the haemovores: they howled in pain as the sound cut straight into their minds like a red-hot knife. They twisted round and backed away from the church door, trying to get away from the agonizing sound.

The Doctor continued to concentrate – *Jo . . . Sarah-Jane . . .* – and the rainbow of sound danced in the air.

* * *

'Takes five against one, does it?'

Sorin's voice rang across the church roof; the other two commandos hauled themselves up behind him. Sorin stared defiantly at the haemovores that held Ace. The haemovores turned to see who the human was who dared mock them.

Sorin pulled at his scarf to reveal his own neck. 'How about a little Cossack blood, eh?' he laughed with scorn.

The haemovores turned and began to advance on Sorin.

'Time for a meal, is it?' he mocked, as the creatures grew closer. Then the smile disappeared from his face, and he raised his Tokarev. 'So eat lead, bloodsuckers!'

A hail of bullets blew the creatures off their feet: the haemovores slithered down the church roof.

'Come on, quick!' Sorin shouted to Ace, as he kicked the frame out of the vestry skylight. 'They're not dead. They'll be back!'

Ace didn't need a second offer, and she scrambled across the roof to the commandos. Already, the haemovores were beginning to crawl back up the roof.

Sorin had knotted a rope round a broken stub of the window frame, and he threw the other end down into the vestry. 'Down there!' he ordered. Ace quickly clambered over the side and disappeared down the rope.

Sorin turned to his two commandos with a smile. 'How about we give one of these leeches a broken heart, boys?' The two commandos grinned back, and Sorin pulled a sharpened wooden stake from his belt.

The nearest haemovore was reaching out towards Sorin, so he edged back a metre or so while the two commandos moved to either side of the haemovore. Sorin waited until he could see that his two colleagues were in position, then he nodded. In a single rapid movement, the two commandos grabbed the haemovore and pinned it down. Sorin raised the stake high above his head, and then drove it down into the heart of the creature.

The haemovore gave out a terrible, tortured cry that seemed to tear through the universe. Sorin pushed down on the stake with all his strength, driving it through the haemovore's body until he felt it hit the slates beneath. The horrible, bloated face of the creature began to twist and change. The skin started to wrinkle and pull back on to the bones as though the creature were growing older by a hundred years every minute. The fleshy lips turned thin and dry and began to crack; the haemovore's whole skeleton began to show through the thin membrane. Then the skin started to smoke and peel away. The creature's cry slowly died away as all its flesh disappeared in smoke.

Soon, all that was left was a smoking skeleton lying in a pool of slime and a charred wooden stake planted between two ribs.

The two commandos stared at it in horror.

'I think he gets the point,' muttered Sorin. 'Come on. We don't have enough stakes for all of them.'

The commandos threw their legs over the edge of the skylight and slipped quickly down the rope.

Ace was staring at the Doctor. He was in some kind of trance and there was a beautiful sound coming from somewhere far away.

The two commandos dropped down the rope, followed by Sorin. The Doctor opened his eyes, and Ace heard the angels' song evaporate into nothingness.

The Doctor turned to Sorin. 'Is there anyone else up there?'

'Only those demons.'

'Right, the way down to the crypt should be clear now. Mr Wainwright, bring that record book with you. We still need it.' The Doctor pushed open the door down to the crypt.

'Wait.' Sorin pulled another stake from his belt. 'I'll go first.'

The Doctor lit the oil lamp while the others followed into the crypt. 'Jam the door shut!' he instructed Sorin, who set to work with the two commandos.

Ace was still puzzled by what she had seen in the vestry. 'That sound you were making – like singing, only it wasn't.'

The Doctor smiled. 'Ah, that. It's an old trick for frightening haemovores.'

'I thought vampies were afraid of crucifixes.'

'It's not the crucifix that scares them. It's the faith of the person holding it. The faith creates a psychic barrier, like I just did. It plays havoc with their telepathic communications! Just a moment . . .' He stopped, as though he'd just remembered something, and then looked at Ace. 'You mean you could hear the sound, too?'

Ace wasn't sure what she was supposed to say. 'Well, yeah.'

'And could you hear anything else when the haemovore were around?'

'Well, there was a sort of squeaking sound.'

'Hmm, yes, that's just the aural backwash. Anything else?'

'Well, there was something sort of funny. But it wasn't anything I could hear.'

'Go on.'

'Well, when I was near the haemovores, I kept getting these strange thoughts. Words at the back of my mind. *Fluid of life* – something like that.'

'Yes, I was picking that up, too.'

'What was doing it?'

'Telepathic communications between the haemovores. It means you're slightly telepathic. Don't worry, it won't do you any harm. But I should steer clear of fundamentalist religious bigots, if I were you. You'll probably find they give you headaches. How are you getting on, Captain?'

'The door's secure.'

'Good.'

But Mr Wainwright wasn't so happy. 'That means we're trapped!'

The Doctor looked at Ace, who was still slightly confused by the recent discovery that she was telepathic. 'Ace?'

Ace tried to concentrate on the new problem. 'Um . . . The old mineshaft in the cellar!'

'Correct!' The Doctor turned to lead the way down to the cellar, but Sorin stopped him.

'I must return to my men.'

Mr Wainwright was horrified at the idea. 'But you've seen those creatures!'

Sorin looked at the young vicar. 'I must try. If I fail, I fail. These two men will stay with you, for protection.'

Ace looked at the Doctor. 'Show him how to make the singing.'

But the Doctor shook his head. 'I can't show him. Either he believes in something – believes absolutely – or he doesn't.'

Sorin stood straight. 'I believe in the Revolution, Doctor.'

'Complete faith, with no doubts?'

Their eyes met. Sorin's expression was determined. 'Go, Doctor. If we meet again, you will have your answer.'

They shook hands briefly, and the Doctor picked up the oil lamp again. He led the way down through the secret door at the far end of the crypt. Ace was the last one to go. She looked back at Sorin for just a moment. She knew she wanted to hold the powerful Russian in her arms for the rest of time. She wanted to feel his warm breath on her cheek and his body tight against hers. She wanted to taste his taste and tumble with him into oblivion.

It was only a moment, then she quickly turned away and hurried through the door after the others.

Sorin looked at the door down from the vestry. The old wood was already beginning to strain and splinter from the creatures on the other side. On his lapel was a red enamel badge in the shape of a star. The insignia in the centre of the badge was a hammer-and-sickle – the international emblem of the working class. He believed, believed passionately, in the right of every worker – whether a worker by hand or by mind – to a fair share in the produce of their work. He took the badge, as the door cracked open and the ghastly creatures began to push through the gaps.

Phyllis and Jean were the first to step through the shattered doorway, followed by other creatures. Sorin held the emblem up and concentrated his mind. He thought of his family, working in the factories and in the offices; he believed in their right to find happiness and fulfilment in their lives. As he concentrated, it seemed as if the emblem was starting to resonate with his thoughts. A single note, sustained pure and true, against the screeching of the haemovores. The creatures screamed in pain and were driven back – back up the stairs, back against the walls.

Sorin walked slowly forwards. He kept his eyes shut, but he sensed the creatures backing away around him. He followed the images in his memory, up the flight of stone stairs and out through the vestry door, and made his way out of the church. He felt the warm air, but still he kept his eyes closed, still concentrating.

He realized suddenly that the screeching sound had gone. He opened his eyes and looked around. He stood alone in the churchyard. Looking back to the church door, he saw a number of haemovores, but he was safe.

He kissed the badge in relief.

The Doctor held up the oil lamp. The entrance to the old mine tunnel had been completely sealed. He turned to the two commandos. 'You two, try to break it open.'

The commandos grabbed a couple of metal implements that had been left behind by the technicians, and started levering at the bricks. The cement hadn't set solid yet, but the bricks would barely move. Ace sighed. 'If you want a job doing properly, get a girl to do it. Out of the way, boys.'

She strode forward and pulled a couple of cans of nitro-nine from her duffle bag. 'Ace,' warned the Doctor.

The commandos stood back, smiling. Ace smiled in return. 'Watch a professional at work, lads.'

She placed the two canisters of Fem-Fresh Maximum Protection Deodorant (Forest Orchid flavour) at the foot of the new brickwork. One of the commandos sniggered. 'No, don't antagonize her,' pleaded the Doctor. 'You'll only make things worse.'

Ace stared at the commandos. 'Two cans of special formula. That should do the trick.'

The commando laughed. The Doctor quickly dragged Mr Wainwright to safety.

Ace smiled sweetly and pulled out the detonator pins.

'And pigs might fly!' mocked the Russian in accented English.

'They do if you shove two hundred grams of nitro up their bum. Four seconds and you're yesterday's breakfast, dog-heap!' And she dived for cover.

On the word nitro, the commandos' faces froze. They hurled themselves behind a large iron tank, landing at exactly the moment the explosives went off.

The commandos were mere novices at the art of nitro-nine. Had they been true aficionados of the craft – as Ace herself was (seventh dan) – they would have appreciated that this one was a classic. A classic. Maximum wallop yielding maximum devastation.

'Wicked!'

The Doctor emerged coughing into the clouds of dust. 'Quick, everyone into the tunnel!' He glared at Ace. 'I'll talk to you later.'

Vershinin was standing on the cliff top when Sorin returned. Vershinin looked around. 'What's happening? It's so dark, but so warm.'

Sorin felt it too. 'There's a storm coming on.'

The Doctor and the others crawled through the dark tunnel. A narrow railway track for carrying small coal wagons ran along the ground, but the roof was no more than a metre and a half high – sometimes less. From the shadows behind them, they heard the screeching of haemovores that followed them.

Ace winced as she cut her leg again on a rock. A dress gave her legs no protection at all. 'How much further to the end?'

The Doctor looked ahead. 'About two or three hundred metres, I think.'

'Those creatures sound as if they're catching up.'

She sat down and let the others pass her while she pulled the old flask from her duffle bag.

'What's the matter?' called the Doctor.

'I'm just trying to get the top off this. It's stuck. Then I can make up some more nitro.'

'This is an enclosed space!' shouted the Doctor in alarm.

'Just a small one, Professor.'

'No.' The Doctor came scrambling back to her, and took the flask before she could do any damage with it.

'You three go ahead,' said one of the commandos. 'We'll stay and slow them down.'

The Doctor looked at them. 'Five minutes, no more. Then you come after us.'

The commando nodded.

The Doctor, Ace and Mr Wainwright continued alone. Suddenly, the Doctor stopped. 'Where did you get this flask?'

'It was just lying around.'

'This is the Viking treasure we were looking for!'

'Oh.'

'And it's what those creatures are after! Why don't you listen to me?'

Ace was about to protest that it wasn't all her fault,

when a voice echoed from the tunnel up ahead. 'Come on, you're almost here,' called Millington. At the same time, they heard gunfire from the tunnel behind them. The haemovores must have encountered the commandos' ambush.

'Go on!' hissed the Doctor. Ace scrambled towards the light she could see ahead. She struggled out through a metal hatch in the side of the tunnel, and found herself in an empty cellar, lit by a single light bulb. Millington was waiting with three naval guards, who helped the Doctor and Mr Wainwright out through the hatch.

'Right, seal it,' ordered Millington.

'No, wait,' explained the Doctor, 'there's two people following us.'

But Millington didn't seem to be listening. 'You're here. That's all I'm interested in. And I'll have those, thank you.' He took the flask from the Doctor and the parish record book which Mr Wainwright was still carrying. Meanwhile, two of the guards closed the old iron shutters across the hatch.

'No, you mustn't,' pleaded the Doctor. 'They'll be killed if we don't let them out. The Russians are on our side.'

The naval guards didn't move.

The two commandos started to bang on the other side of the shutters.

Mr Wainwright turned to Millington. 'Please, commander. Those creatures, they're inhuman.'

'So's he,' muttered Ace.

Millington's mind was trapped in the past. 'Many years ago, when I was just a chief petty officer on board ship, we had an explosion in an engine room. We had to seal it off to save the ship – keep the flames restricted to one section, you know. We could hear men screaming behind the bulkheads for nearly an hour. Eventually, the screaming stopped. You do understand, don't you?'

The Doctor didn't reply.

Document IV

The First Contest of Fenric

From Ancient Arabian Tales, *translated by Sir William Judson, published 1847.*

The Story of 'Alee Sheyr the Traveller and the Princess Leylà

There was, in ancient times, a Kaleefeh[1] named Sháh-Zemán, who ruled from the White City; and he had a single daughter named Leylà. The Kaleefeh Sháh-Zemán was very fond of Leylà; and he gave her jewels and silks and hand-maidens; but always she was sad. And because the Kaleefeh so loved his only daughter, he resolved that she should never marry any man who could not make her happy.

Now, the Princess Leylà was more beautiful than the full moon in the night sky, and news of her great beauty did spread across land and sea; and three Princes journeyed from distant islands to seek the hand of the Kaleefeh Sháh-Zemán's daughter. The Kaleefeh summoned the three Princes to stand before

---

[1] The kaleefeh (or caliph) was the ruler of a city or territory.

him; and he said, if you would marry my only daughter, then you must each give her a present, to win her heart. Whichever of you is successful, and makes her happy with his gift, may marry her; but those of you who fail, shall have your head struck off.

As he spoke these words, there was a commotion outside; and the Kaleefeh said to his Vezeer[2], What is this noise that disturbs us.

There is a poor Traveller outside, replied the Vezeer; and he would also beg the hand of your daughter, the Princess Leylà, in marriage.

Let him come before me, ordered the Kaleefeh.

So the Traveller was brought before the Kaleefeh Sháh-Zemán. Who are you, demanded the Kaleefeh, that asks to marry my only daughter?

My name is 'Alee Sheyr, replied the man, and I am a poor Traveller; but I have heard that the Princess Leylà is more beautiful than the morning sun, but very sad. I have neither palace nor eunuchs; but I think that I can make her happy; and I would like to marry her.

The Kaleefeh Sháh-Zemán's advisers were angry that a poor Traveller should make such a request. O master, they cried, let us execute him for his temerity.

No, replied the Kaleefeh, I have promised that my daughter shall marry the man who can win her heart. Let 'Alee Sheyr the Traveller make his gift to my daughter; and if he shall make her happy, then may he marry her; but if he should fail, then must he die.

So the three Princes and 'Alee Sheyr the Traveller were taken before the Princess Leylà, to make their gifts. The first Prince, from the Islands of Khálidán,[3]

[2] A vezeer (or vizier) was the chief adviser to a kaleefeh.
[3] Khálidán is most likely a corruption of El-Khálidát or El-Khálidetán, which mean, in Arabic, the Fortunate Islands. These are known to us as the Canaries.

stepped forward, and presented the Princess with a great casket made entirely of gold; and inside, it was filled with diamonds and pearls and ivory; and he said, O Princess Leylà, I have brought you greater riches than any Princess before you. If you will consent to marry me, I will give you even greater wealth.

The Princess saw the great treasure, which the Prince from the Islands of Khálidán had laid at her feet; but she knew that she was still sad; and she said, O Prince, you bring me the treasure of great riches; but I do not love you.

So, the Prince from the Islands of Khálidán was taken away; and his head was struck off. Then the second Prince, from the Interior Islands of China[4], stepped forward; and he presented her with twelve small jars; and the jars were filled with the most delicate scents and perfumes that ever were made. If you will marry me, I shall set one hundred men to the task of gathering even rarer delights.

The Princess perfumed her body with the fragrances, which the Prince from the Interior Islands of China had brought for her; but she knew that she was still sad; and she said, O Prince, you bring me the treasure of rare perfumes; but I do not love you.

So, the Prince from the Interior Islands of China was taken away; and his head was struck off. Then the third Prince, from the Furthest Island of Dhógs[5], stepped forward with a most wondrous animal, which

[4] It should be observed, that the Arabic word for island (jezeereh) may also mean peninsula, or even country.

[5] Although other references to this place can be found in literature of the period, making mention of its tremendous wealth, archaeologists have been unable to locate the site, and it is now thought that the place never existed.

had the head of a lion, the wings of an eagle, and the tail of a peacock; and he said, O Princess Leylà, I have travelled many months and suffered great hardships journeying along the Central Way from the Furthest Island of Dhógs to the White City; and I have brought you a strange and wonderful animal. If you will marry me, I shall give you such animals as you cannot even imagine.

The Princess looked on the extraordinary animal, which the Prince from the Furthest Island of Dhógs had brought her; but she knew that she was still sad; and she said, O Prince, you bring me the treasure of a wonderful beast; but I do not love you.

So, the Prince from the Furthest Island of Dhógs was taken away and his head was struck off. Then 'Alee Sheyr the Traveller stepped forward, and he took from his sack a square of wood and some small carved figures[6]; and he said, O Princess Leylà, I have no possessions which I can give to you, apart from this, a game with which I amuse myself on my journeys. It is only a small gift, but I would like to tell you the story of how I came by it.

The Princess looked at the game, with its marked board and the small carved figures; and she said, Tell me your story, O 'Alee Sheyr the Traveller.

So 'Alee Sheyr said, This game was made by another traveller, named El-Dok'Tár[7], who lived many years ago, during the House of El-Sásánian[8]. At this time, the Great City in Bilád er-Room[9] was

[6] From the description, this would seem to be a game of chess.

[7] The name El-Dok'Tár denotes a traveller who has gained much wisdom durin the course of his journeys.

[8] The dynasty of El-Sásánian lasted from AD 202 until AD 636.

[9] The name Bilád er-Room is applied by some Arab geographers to territories now constituting modern Greece and European

137

tyrannized by an evil Jinnee[10] named Aboo-Fenrán[11], who caused great storms and turned men's hands to killing and war. In particular, the Jinnee took evil pleasure in setting traps for men, and seeing them ensnared. The Prince El-Amjad went to the sandy plains outside the City, to make a bargain with Aboo-Fenrán, that Aboo-Fenrán should leave the Great City in peace. I will leave the Great City, replied Aboo-Fenrán, on condition that you give to me the first thing that you name on returning to the Palace.

The Prince agreed to this; and he returned to the Palace, thinking to name some small piece of treasure. But, as the Prince El-Amjad passed through the Palace gates, Aboo-Fenrán sent a mighty wind through the Palace. The wind caught the Prince's youngest daughter, who was waiting for her father's return; and it blew her to the ground. Without thinking, the Prince El-Amjad called out his youngest daughter's name in alarm; and then he realized what he had done; for, in calling out his youngest daughter's name, he had been caught in Aboo-Fenrán's trap. When Aboo-Fenrán sent a messenger to claim his prize, the Prince tried to deceive him; and he sent a large chest of gold, saying, This was the first thing that I named, when I returned to the Palace.

But when Aboo-Fenrán saw that the Prince El-Amjad was not going to hand over his youngest daughter, Aboo-Fenrán redoubled his evil; and the

---

Turkey, but by others to parts of Asia Minor. I believe that the reference here to the Great City means present-day Constantinople.

[10] A jinnee (or genie) was a supernatural spirit, often evil.

[11] In one of the fables from the *Thousand and One Nights*, Aboo-Fenrán is used as the appellation of an evil wolf.

people of the Great City wept in suffering. The Prince El-Amjad sent out word that he would make a gift of one half-share of his treasures to the man who could defeat Aboo-Fenrán. Many men tried; but the evil powers of Aboo-Fenrán were too great; and all the men died.

Now, it happened that, at this time, El-Dok'Tár arrived in the Great City; and he asked why the people were crying; and he was told of the evil Jinnee Aboo-Fenrán. So, El-Dok'Tár went to the Prince El-Amjad; and he said, O Prince, if I defeat Aboo-Fenrán, then must you give me whatever I ask.

The Prince El-Amjad replied, I have offered a half-share of my treasures to the man who can defeat Aboo-Fenrán.

Nevertheless, insisted El-Dok'Tár, if I defeat Aboo-Fenrán, you must give me whatsoever I demand in return. If you do not, I shall destroy your Palace; for if I can defeat Aboo-Fenrán, then my powers must be even greater than his.

With a heavy heart, the Prince El-Amjad agreed; for he knew that El-Dok'Tár would demand El-Amjad's entire palace and also all his daughters in payment. I shall require a weapon, said El-Dok'Tár. I shall need a small knife with a sharp edge.

The Prince and his advisers begged El-Dok'Tár to take a larger weapon; but El-Dok'Tár refused. So, they gave him a sharp knife; and El-Dok'Tár set off for the sandy plains outside the Great City, where Aboo-Fenrán was busy making dust storms. O Aboo-Fenrán! called El-Dok'Tár, I have come to challenge you!

The Jinnee turned his evil red eyes to look at El-Dok'Tár; and he called down, Who are you, that dares challenge me?

I am El-Dok'Tár, replied the brave Traveller.

Do you know who I am? demanded Aboo-Fenrán in a terrible voice.

I know you, O Aboo-Fenrán, shouted El-Dok'Tár. You are the Dark One, who is come from the time before Time; as I am Light, so are you Dark; and I shall banish you to the Shadows.

At first, Aboo-Fenrán did not reply; but presently he said, So, El-Dok'Tár; as you are Light, so am I Dark. I think that I know your true identity. I think, that you also come from the time before Time. How do you propose to defeat me, then?

A contest, Aboo-Fenrán, replied El-Dok'Tár. We shall battle, the forces of Dark against the forces of Light.

Where are your forces? laughed Aboo-Fenrán. There is no one here but you!

These are my forces, shouted El-Dok'Tár; and he picked some small, white bones from the sands; and, with his sharp knife, he quickly carved them into small figures. Then he took some pieces of black charcoal; and he carved those into small figures, also; and he placed them all on a wooden table, marked in squares. These figures shall be our armies! shouted El-Dok'Tár. Play the contest of traps, Aboo-Fenrán!

So, for forty days and forty nights, El-Dok'Tár and Aboo-Fenrán played the contest of traps, without either of them being able to win the game; until, on the fortieth night, El-Dok'Tár said, Aboo-Fenrán, you have one move remaining, with which to defeat me. If you do not, then I shall defeat you with my next move.

How do I know that you are not lying? asked Aboo-Fenrán.

There is only one way to find out, replied El-Dok'Tár. If you can not defeat me in one move, then you will discover whether or not I am lying; but I shall help you. I shall tell you that I can see one move which you can make that will defeat me; but it is one move, and one move only. I shall leave the flask[12] here, while you consider your move.

Aboo-Fenrán looked at the pieces; but he could not see the winning move. For another forty days and forty nights, he sat at the table. Every morning, El-Dok'Tár would return to the sandy plains, to see if Aboo-Fenrán had made his move; and every morning, Aboo-Fenrán would make the same plea: Show me the winning move, I beg you.

El-Dok'Tár said nothing, however. He merely returned each day; and he saw that Aboo-Fenrán's powers were growing weaker and the light in the Jinnee's evil red eyes was growing fainter; and on the forty-first morning, El-Dok'Tár said, Aboo-Fenrán, you have failed to discover the winning move. I, therefore, claim victory as mine; and I banish you to the Shadows.

You may have won the contest, replied Aboo-Fenrán; but you will never banish me to the Shadows!

El-Dok'Tár picked up the flask; and he said, Aboo-Fenrán, this flask does not come from the Great City, and it does not contain fragrant oils. I have carried this flask with me on my long travels; for this flask contains the Seven Shadows from the time before Time. Eighty days ago, you were strong; and you could have resisted me; but my contest has weakened

[12] The Arabic word matrah means a flask or jar, used for perfumes and the like. Here, the perfume would be used for its refreshing qualities during the game.

your powers. You can not resist me any longer. Aboo-Fenrán, I banish you to the Seven Shadows!

As El-Dok'Tár spoke these final words, the flask suddenly glowed with a strange, green light. Aboo-Fenrán struggled to flee; but the green light drew him back. As the green light grew stronger, so Aboo-Fenrán shrank smaller; and he was drawn right inside the flask itself. Once Aboo-Fenrán was gone, El-Dok'Tár placed the stopper in the flask; and the green glow disappeared.

El-Dok'Tár returned to the Palace; and he said to the Prince El-Amjad, I have defeated the evil Jinnee, Aboo-Fenrán, and trapped him in this flask. Now you must give me whatsoever I ask.

Very well, replied the Prince; although I know that you will demand my entire palace and all my daughters.

Not so, replied El-Dok'Tár. You have an Abyssinian slave-girl, named Zeleekhà. I ask that she be released, and given to me; so that she may accompany me on my travels.

The Prince El-Amjad was startled that El-Dok'Tár demanded no more than a slave-girl; and he ordered that Zeleekhà be released, and handed over. El-Dok'Tár left the Palace, with his new companion; and he was never seen again.

Zeleekhà, the former slave-girl, returned two years later; and she went to the Prince El-Amjad in his Palace. She told the Prince stories of her adventures with El-Dok'Tár. She told of how they had flown among the stars in the night sky; she told of journeys through distant lands on distant worlds; and she told of creatures more strange than the strangest of dreams. Finally, Zeleekhà gave to the Prince El-Amjad an old flask; and she said, El-Dok'Tár asked

142

me to give this to you. He asks that you hide it away; and that you never break it open; for the evil Jinnee, Aboo-Fenrán, is trapped inside; and if he should escape, he would be more powerful than ever.

So, the Prince El-Amjad took the flask; and he hid it; and nothing more was ever heard of Aboo-Fenrán.

And that is how the pieces of this game were made, concluded 'Alee Sheyr the Traveller. They were given to me when I journeyed through Bilád er-Room, by an old man who found them on the sandy plains where El-Dok'Tár defeated the evil Jinnee. Princess Leylà looked at the game which the poor Traveller offered her; and she said, O 'Alee Sheyr, you do not bring me great riches, or delicate perfumes, or wonderful creatures; but you bring me a treasure more valuable than all of these; for your story has made me happy, which none of these other treasures could do! If you will tell me one story every night after our marriage, then I shall love you and be happy! And the Kaleefeh Sháh-Zemán saw that his only daughter was smiling and happy, so he consented for her to marry 'Alee Sheyr the Traveller.

For a story may contain all the treasures, and all the happiness, of the world.

Chronicle V

Wind and Water, Earth and Fire

1

The commandos of the Red Army's Special Operations Brigade scouted low through the undergrowth until they reached the perimeter fence of the North Yorkshire Signals Camp.

Sorin turned to Vershinin. 'You stay here. If I give you the signal to abort the mission, get out immediately. And if I'm not back in ten minutes, abort the mission anyway. Don't wait for me, do you understand?'

Vershinin nodded.

'Right, go.' Sorin motioned the others to disperse.

Once they had disappeared, he looked towards the main gate of the camp. Marines had taken the place of naval guards, and the security had been strengthened. But the war seemed unimportant now – a squabble between men who had no knowledge of the dark creatures that threatened them. Sorin had to convince the base commander that unless they fought the evil together they would all die.

He stood up and walked towards the main gate.

The marines' rifles followed him, but Sorin's eyes were fixed on the huts in the camp. He stopped a few yards from the gate, and called. 'Commander Millington, I want to talk with you – officer to officer!'

The clatter of relays and the teleprinter filled the decryption room. Millington handed the old flask to Dr Judson. 'We have it, Judson! At last! I said it would be brought to us. The legends shall come true. Take it. Release the power!'

There was a rapid knock at the door, and Bates hurried in. 'Sir, the house guests! They're here!'

Millington stared in disbelief. 'What?'

'The house guests! There's one outside – wants to talk with you.'

Millington looked briefly at the flask, and then strode from the room.

He emerged from the hut, and looked round.

'We must talk, Commander Millington,' called a voice.

Millington saw a Red Army captain standing in the main drive. He walked slowly towards the Russian. 'I'm afraid you have me at a disadvantage. You seem to know my name, but I don't know yours.' He smiled as he heard the click of rifles. 'However, that hardly seems to matter now. You will tell your men to put down their weapons and surrender.'

Sorin was trapped, but his real fear was of the creatures. 'Commander, you must listen to me. This camp is in great danger, a danger you cannot even begin to imagine.'

'Your men, captain.'

Sorin half turned and shouted back to his unit. 'Lay down your weapons, and come in peacefully . . . like the wolves of winter!'

145

The wolves! Millington froze.

'Come on! Pull back!' hissed Vershinin. 'That's the code word! Let's get out of here!'

'They're out there!' ordered Millington. 'Find them!'

Bates organized his men. 'C unit with Sergeant McAvoy, cover the church!' he barked. 'A and B units with me, spreading out through the woods!'

'No, wait!' Millington thought of the Ultima machine and the flask. 'We can't afford to weaken the camp's defences. Dr Judson's work must be protected! I want the whole camp on status azure, captain! And put the Russian under twenty-four hour guard!'

'Sir!'

Millington spun round and marched off towards his office. Bates barked orders behind him. The Doctor was standing in the doorway of a hut as Millington marched past.

'You still don't understand, do you, Commander?'

Millington glared at the Doctor. 'This camp is now locked up tight, Doctor. Nothing – absolutely nothing – will get in or out.'

'Ah yes, status azure. A suicide defence pattern in which a military installation is divided into sectors. Should the enemy penetrate any sector, the defensive personnel will destroy the whole sector, themselves included.'

'You seem to know a great deal about the defence of military establishments – rather more than a scientist ought to know. If you're still alive tomorrow, I intend to find out who you really are.'

'Those creatures aren't going to be stopped by your status azure! They devour humans just like humans eat fruit!'

'I doubt if any creature can walk through iron shutters.'

'They can weld metal beneath the sea with their bare hands.'

The Doctor held out his strange coral-like piece of metalwork.

Down in the cellar, the iron shutters that sealed the old mine tunnel were beginning to bubble – slowly dissolving from an acid attack.

Ace peered into the Wrens' quarters. She wasn't sure if the sound she heard was a woman laughing or a woman crying.

Kathleen was sitting on her bunk; her suitcase rested on the floor.

'Kathleen? You all right?'

But Kathleen continued sobbing.

Ace sat quietly beside her, and put an arm round Kathleen. 'What's the matter?' she whispered gently. 'Whatever it is, I'll help. It'll be all right.'

She looked down, and saw that Kathleen was clutching a piece of paper. Slowly she pulled it from Kathleen's warm fingers and uncrumpled it. The paper was an official telegram from the Ministry of War. As Ace read the words, she felt the grief that filled Kathleen.

To: Mrs F. W. Dudman, North Yorkshire Signals Camp.

It is with deepest sorrow that I write to inform you that the ship on which your husband Frank William Dudman was serving was struck by enemy torpedoes. Your husband was trapped in the fire and has been listed as missing, presumed dead. Please accept our sincere condolences.

Ace couldn't read any further.

'Kathleen . . . I'm sorry.'

She put her arms round Kathleen and held her. There was nothing Ace could do or say to ease the sobs of grief. Nothing that could bring back the only thing in the world that Kathleen wanted. Nothing that could take away the cold words of the telegram. Nothing.

So she just held Kathleen in her arms, because that was all she could do.

'As long as it takes,' she whispered.

The rotors hummed and the relays maintained a constant clicking, but the teleprinter sat waiting now. The Ultima machine was near the end of its crazed dance through the possibilities of history. Metres and metres of teleprinter tape lay discarded on the floor, a single weft through the vast genealogical weave of the human race.

Dr Judson sat waiting. He sensed that he was on the threshold of something huge and unimaginable. A doorway that was about to open – a doorway to some black universe full of terrible powers. And a figure with evil red eyes stood waiting in the darkness beyond the door. Waiting for the key that would unlock the door.

The machine was the key; the names were the levers in the lock. One lever, one lever more . . .

Empty of feeling and drained of strength, Kathleen had fallen asleep. But Ace sat by her, watching her sleep. Anger grew inside her as she watched.

This was what it came down to – *please accept our sincere condolences* from a nameless functionary of the Ministry of War. Words on paper that destroyed a woman's life and took away a baby's father. Adventures in history books that filled thousands of fields with dark, empty gravestones stretching as far as the eye could see. Destroyed unknown thousands of womens' lives and took away countless thousands of babies' fathers. Who was playing these games with human souls? Who had the right to destroy like this?

She looked up, full of anger.

She found him in the bunk room.

The Doctor saw the anger burning in Ace's eyes.

'You know what's going on, don't you?' she hissed.

The Doctor stood. His face was dark and full of ancient powers.

'Yes,' he said, and turned to the shadows.

'You always know! You just can't be bothered to tell anyone!' Ace's anger flared. 'Like it's some kind of game, and only you know the rules! You knew all about the inscriptions being a computer program, but you didn't tell me! You know all about that old bottle, but you're not telling me! Am I so stupid?'

'No, that's not it.' The Doctor's voice was warning and full of danger, but Ace was possessed by her fury.

'Why? I want to know!'

The Doctor turned on her. Hatred filled his face, and his voice trembled with rage. 'Evil! Evil from the dawn of time!'

'What do you mean? I want to know!'

'Stop asking me these questions!'

'Tell me!' Ace hurled her fury at the Doctor, and suddenly she saw it in his eyes. A momentary glimpse of his birth.

'The dawn of time!' cried the Doctor, as the pain shot through him again. 'The beginning of all beginnings! Two forces only: good and evil! Then chaos! Time is born! Matter, space! The universe cries out like a newborn!' His eyes were consumed with torment. 'Please don't make me . . .'

Ace grabbed him by the shoulders. 'You must. You must tell me what happened.'

'The peace is lost for ever! The two forces shatter as the universe explodes outwards! Only echoes remain. But somehow, somehow the evil force survives. The echoes coalesce. An intelligence forms. Evil! Pure evil!'

The Doctor's final cry tore through the quiet. He threw out his arms to clutch at the heavens. The violence knocked Ace sideways and she spun into a wall, but just as the Doctor was about to fall, he caught himself. His fists closed tight and his face clenched as he struggled to fight the frenzy inside him. He trembled as he fought to control the torment and banish it to the night. Finally he was still, his body caught in the air.

Slowly he lowered his arms, and opened his eyes. The ancient power had settled about him once more. He looked at Ace.

'And that's Fenric?' she asked.

'No, that's just Millington's name for it.' His voice was calm. 'The evil itself has no name. Trapped inside the flask, like an evil genie in a bottle.'

'Can we fight it?'

'We need to recover the flask.'

'We have to release Captain Sorin.'

'How?'

'I can distract the guard.'

The Doctor looked at Ace.

'Doctor, I'm not a little girl.'

The air outside was warm and humid.

In the guard post, Leigh loosened his collar and opened the window wider, but there was no relief from the still, sticky air. A trickle of sweat ran down his face, and he saw a movement in the doorway.

The young woman was leaning agains the doorframe, her mouth hiding the possibility of a smile. Leigh turned to her. 'You looking for someone?'

The young woman balanced the answer on her lips before replying. 'No. Maybe . . . Are you . . . ?'

Leigh grinned.

Then she disappeared. Leigh followed her outside, into the warm, saturated day. She was leaning back against the hut with her eyes closed. Beads of sweat gathered on her face.

'Too hot,' murmured Ace. 'Clothes sticking to me, sticking to my skin, hot, damp . . .'

'If they're too sticky, you know what to do.'

He grinned.

Lazily, she opened an eye and looked at him. 'The question is . . . is he making all the right moves or only going through the motions?'

She turned listlessly and disappeared again. He followed her.

The Doctor took his chance.

Even here in the shadows, the warm damp stuck close. He leaned in to her. 'What are you doing here?' he whispered.

'Have to move faster than that if you want to keep up with me. Faster than light.'

'Faster than a second hand on a watch?'

151

'Much faster. We're hardly moving yet. Not even cruising speed. Sometimes I travel so fast I don't exist any more.' She closed her eyes and knew the feeling again. The momentary annihilation of all existence except her own, and the deep, sweet knowledge of her own being. The brief joining of life and death.

She turned to look at him.

'What can you see?' he asked.

She felt the stirrings from deep within. Dangerous undercurrents, bringing things to the surface. She turned quickly away. 'I can't stay,' she insisted.

'You promised.'

'I can't.' And she was gone.

Mr Wainwright stood watching as the metal shutters dissolved in front of him. Already inhuman hands were pushing through, as the acid holes in the shutters grew larger. The screeching sound was horrible, but Mr Wainwright stood firm.

The two girls were the first to push through into the cellar. They looked up and saw the young vicar, and a deadly smile twisted in the corners of their red lips.

Slowly Mr Wainwright raised his Bible in front of him.

'The book won't do you any good,' mocked Jean. 'You don't believe.'

'We'll see,' challenged Mr Wainwright, as he grasped the book tight and closed his eyes. He concentrated on his faith – his two-thousand-year-old faith. After two thousand years, there must be truth in it. There was good and there was sin. A two-thousand-year-old truth – he must cling to it and believe in it: no half-truths; no compromises with a complex and changing world – just good and sin.

Beyond his hearing, a sound began to swell. A strident chorus that pierced the creatures' thoughts. Jean and Phyllis gasped in pain.

'It's not true,' cried Phyllis. 'You don't believe.'

'Look at us!' shouted Jean. 'Where's the good in us?'

Mr Wainwright grasped the book ever more strongly, and kept his eyes tight shut. He mustn't look up, mustn't look at all. He must never open his eyes again. Just concentrate on the truth. 'Good and sin. I believe . . .'

'Look at us!'

He couldn't help himself. He looked. And the two-thousand-year-old lie shattered.

The chorus failed, and the creatures turned on the young vicar. Jean smiled cruelly. 'We said we'd come back for you.'

Her nails glittered like blades in the night.

Ace caught up with the Doctor and Sorin as they ran across the compound towards the decryption room. The warm, heavy air had drawn even closer, and dark clouds filled the sky. Sweat ran down their faces. The storm was almost upon them.

'Quick!' shouted the Doctor.

'How are we going to stop Fenric?' called Ace.

'Evil needs a body. It hasn't found one yet.'

The decryption room was dark as the storm gathered outside, but the machine's relays went on clicking, searching for the final name. Dr Judson sat waiting, watching, while Millington paced irritably behind him. Nurse Crane was tense with fear. Something terrible was about to happen, she knew it.

Suddenly, the teleprinter began to clatter. Everyone

153

froze as a short burst of print appeared on the tape, and the teleprinter spat out the final few letters. Then the entire machine went dead. The relays fell silent, the rotors whirred to a halt, and the printer was still.

Millington stared dumbly at the dark machine. 'What's happened, Judson?'

Dr Judson leaned forward to look at the final word on the teleprinter tape.

INGIGER.

What did it mean? He reached to take the tape, but as he touched it, a huge green spark flashed from the heart of the machine. The air crackled with the buzz of a massive energy surge, and the spark engulfed the crippled scientist. The ancient flask shattered, and Dr Judson's body was thrown across the room.

A colossal bolt of lightning ripped the sky over Maidens' Point and the storm broke.

Beneath the waters, among the swirling undercurrents, a figure stirred.

Now is the time, Ingiger! After a thousand years, now is the time!

Mr Wainwright lay dead in the cellar. The monstrous faces of the creatures shone deathly pale in the dark, and more of them continued to emerge from the old mine tunnel.

The flash of lightning from outside illuminated the decryption room as the Doctor and Ace burst through the door, followed by Sorin. The Doctor looked in horror at what he saw.

The body of Dr Judson lay dead on the ground. Millington stood by the window, staring outwards;

154

and Nurse Crane knelt by the body. She reached to move the body.

'Don't touch him!' cried the Doctor. 'Don't touch anything!'

Nurse Crane looked up. 'But he's an invalid. He can't even stand unless I help him.'

She didn't understand. The Doctor looked down on her pityingly. 'He's dead,' he said gently.

'Now is the time,' Millington turned slowly. In a flash of lightning his face was filled with evil. 'The chains of Fenric are shattered! The gods have lost the final battle! The Dead Men's Ship has slipped its moorings, and the Great Ash Tree itself trembles to its very roots!'

'We're too late!' cried Ace. 'Fenric's found a body! It's him!'

Millington swung round to stare at her, then he turned to the body on the floor and whispered in horror, 'Fenric!'

The body moved. An evil strength filled the limbs – limbs that had been crippled for twenty years. The body of Dr Judson slowly rose from the floor and stood before them. For a moment it didn't move, feeling its new strength, then it opened its eyes.

They glowed red in the darkened room, seeking someone out. They found the Doctor. Fenric smiled. 'You left me trapped in the shadow dimensions. Trapped for seventeen centuries. Seventeen centuries in which to prepare for this moment. And now I have a body again.' The eyes burned with hatred. 'We play the contest again, Time Lord.'

His eyes blinked shut and a huge wind whipped through the room. The hurricane smashed windows, upturned furniture, and threw everyone against the walls. Then it was gone. Only the storm raged outside.

Fenric had disappeared.

155

2

The door burst open and Bates rushed in, followed by Leigh.

'Shoot them!' ordered Millington, pointing to the Doctor, Ace and Sorin.

Bates hesitated. 'What for?'

'Because I order you to!' snapped Millington. 'For treason.'

Leigh was already shoving the Doctor and Ace out of the decryption room.

Outside, the sky was black and the rain poured down in a tropical storm. The air turned white with a flash of lightning and a huge crack of thunder burst overhead.

'You men, form a firing squad!' shouted Leigh to a group of marines as they ran from the guard post. He turned on the Doctor and Ace. 'Against the wall!' he ordered.

Bates was marching Sorin at gunpoint to join them. The Doctor tried to plead with him for Ace's life. 'You don't need to kill her.'

But Bates didn't want to hear. 'Let's just get it over with.' In his heart, he knew the little man and the girl weren't spies, but an order had been given. He turned to Leigh and the firing squad. 'Ready!'

The firing squad raised their rifles. Bates strode away to a safe distance. The Doctor's voice followed him through the wind and rain. 'She's only a child.'

But Bates refused to hear.

'Killing us won't stop the creatures!' called Sorin.

'Aim!'

Ace knew she was going to die, and only one thing filled her mind – one last thing she must say. 'Mum, I'm sorry!' she cried into the storm.

'Fire!'

At that moment, an explosion burst the ground where the firing party stood, and echoed through the storm. A second grenade spun through the air, and the rapid crackle of Tokarev semi-automatics erupted from the perimeter fence. The explosion of the second grenade rocked the camp.

'Grenades!' shouted Bates, as the marines ran for cover. Three marines lay motionless in the mud.

'Captain! Over here!' Vershinin's voice rang through the confusion.

'Come on!' shouted Sorin, pulling the Doctor and Ace towards the guard post. Their feet slipped in the mud as they ducked low and ran.

The Russian commandos had already pushed forward from the perimeter fence and taken cover behind the guard post. Two small groups were now breaking for nearby buildings. The marines and naval guards had opened fire on the commandos' positions, but the Russians were firmly established.

Vershinin took a pair of chain-cutters and snapped off Sorin's manacles.

'What took you so long?' demanded Sorin.

Vershinin grinned. 'I thought you seemed to have it all under control, captain.'

A rush of wind filled the cellar. When it disappeared, Fenric was standing in front of the haemovores. He looked round, his eyes blinking a fiery red. 'I was expecting only one creature. And I was hoping for

157

something a little more, well, Aryan. No matter. Let the Ancient One approach me.'

His eyes scanned the creatures for the one he sought.

'Where is the Ancient One?' he demanded angrily. He stepped over the dead body of Mr Wainwright, his eyes fixed on Jean and Phyllis.

'He waits,' replied Phyllis.

'He waits? He waits? Has he no sense of occasion! I want him here! Now!'

'As you command,' the two girls replied obediently.

They turned to the tunnel entrance. At that moment, the door down from the laboratory was thrown open and two marines opened fire into the cellar. The bullets ripped through the girls' bodies: the force knocked the two girls back a few steps, but they didn't fall. The bullet holes gaped white and bloodless in their flesh.

The two girls looked up. The marines stood frozen with fear.

Jean raised an arm and pointed at the marines. The other creatures began to advance on the men. In desperation, the marines fired more rounds into the creatures, but to no effect.

The creatures' nails glittered in the dark once again.

Fenric smiled.

The Russians had taken cover inside the guard post, and were keeping up a constant gunfire from the windows. The crackle of guns spat through the hurricane outside.

Ace stood silently in the corner.

The Doctor moved beside her. 'What was it you said?'

'When?'

'Outside. You shouted something.'

Mum, I'm sorry!

'Oh, nothing. Just something.'

'Your mum,' persisted the Doctor.

Ace turned angrily on him. 'Look, stop playing games with me!'

'We've all been playing games. Fenric's games. Playing his games and walking into his traps.' The Doctor's face was dark. 'I must do it. I must play the game to the end this time.'

'What game?'

'A very simple game. A game of chess. But I can't play without any pieces!'

'If we could get into Commander Millington's office, we could take his set.'

Sorin turned to them. 'A chess set? We came here to steal the Ultima machine. A chess set is no problem.'

He indicated to two commandos. 'Create a diversion. Make it big.'

The two commandos said nothing, but picked up two light backpacks and slipped out into the storm.

Millington sat in his office as the storm raged outside. Only the glow of a small desk-lamp lit his features as he gazed on the chess figures.

'And the battlefield shall stretch a hundred leagues,' he murmured in his madness. 'And at the end of the day, not one living thing shall be left alive. The ancient enemies shall seek each other out, and all shall die.'

Audrey cried at the noise outside the hut. Kathleen held the baby close and looked round in terror. She tried to sing to Audrey.

'When the bough breaks,
    The cradle will fall.
Down will come baby,
    cradle and all.'

One of the two commandos ran away from a small hut that had *Generator Room* stencilled on the door. He ducked beneath the gunfire and hurled himself into the mud, just as two kilogrammes of stick TNT detonated and ripped through the hut.

The small desk lamp flickered, and went dark.

Millington looked up. He must take charge of the battle.

Marines and naval guards were firing in complete confusion. Leigh grabbed the field telephone. 'Captain! They've taken out the generator!'

Bates, in the command room, snapped back into his handset. 'There's only a dozen of them! What the hell's going on out there?'

The second commando leaned forward, and clipped through the telephone wires.

'Sergeant? Sergeant . . . ?'

Bates flicked the switch a few times, but the line was dead.

'Now!' ordered Sorin, and threw open the door. 'Go!'

The commandos surged through the door and disappeared into the storm.

'Come on!' called Sorin to the Doctor and Ace.

The wind and rain lashed their faces as they followed the commandos. Vershinin was leading the commandos in a zig-zag manoeuvre across the compound, drawing the British fire.

Sorin turned to the Doctor and pointed towards a gap between two huts. 'You've got a clear path through the British positions!' he shouted.

'Come on!' the Doctor called to Ace.

Leigh had organized a handful of men out of the confusion and was about to fall back and defend the decryption room.

'Forget the machine!' shouted Millington. 'Establish new positions, sergeant! We must secure the lab!'

The waves pounded on the shore and the wind whipped the rain into the faces of Jean and Phyllis as they stood facing the sea. Slowly they raised their arms.

'You are summoned. You must obey.'

The waters of Maidens' Point thrashed with the raging undercurrents, and a dark figure broke the surface. Ingiger, more monstrous than any other of the haemovores, rose from the deep, and began to stride towards the girls. Around its body, a network of filaments linked dozens of small metal objects in the creature's shiny coral chain mail.

The marines secured new positions around the old pit building. Millington turned to Bates. 'Hold these positions! Use whatever weapons are needed!'

'Sir!'

Millington disappeared into the laboratory.

Inside, Fenric stood among the endless rows of chemical bombs, listening to the gunfire outside – a demon priest in his cathedral.

'Ah . . . the sound of dying!' he whispered, as his

161

eyes glowed bright. 'When it comes to death, quantity is so much more satisfying than quality!'

Millington stared at him. 'The final battle . . .'

Fenric turned irritably on Millington. 'Don't interrupt me when I'm eulogizing! Where is the Time Lord?'

'Time Lord?'

'The one you call Doctor.'

'I had him shot.'

'I can see you've never been burdened with great intelligence,' scorned Fenric. Then his voice turned hard. 'For seventeen centuries I was trapped in the shadow dimensions, because of him. He pulled bones from the desert sands and carved them into chess pieces. He challenged me to solve his puzzle. I failed. I shall see him kneel in front of me before I let him die.'

'Ready!'

The marines pulled the pins from their grenades. A small yellow outline was stencilled on the base of each grenade: the skull and crossbones of chemical weapons.

'Now!' ordered Bates.

The marines hurled the grenades towards the Russian positions. As they landed, a green gas began to ooze from the grenades. It swirled in the wind, and wrapped itself around the Russians.

Sorin felt his skin burn as the caustic mist blew over him.

'Gas!' he called to Vershinin and the others. 'Everybody out!'

Already the acid mist was scorching his lungs, and he gasped as he staggered back towards the perimeter fence. His eyes were on fire, and he collapsed in the mud behind the dead body of a naval guard. Vershinin fell beside him moments later, every breath of fresh air he took shot knives of pain through his lungs.

'The others,' gasped Sorin.

They looked up. In the swirling green fog, they could just make out the figures of their comrades, screaming in pain. Sorin tried to stagger to his feet. 'We must help them!'

'No,' Vershinin grabbed Sorin and pulled him down into the mud again. 'There's nothing we can do, captain.'

They watched as their screaming comrades fell to the ground, writhing in agony. Then the screaming stopped: the bodies lay motionless.

Bates looked across the compound. The gunfire had stopped; only the storm continued to roar. And as the winds blew away the green gas, he saw dozens of bodies lying in the mud. It was impossible to tell which were British and which were Russian.

Millington stood alongside him.

'Are they Russians?' asked Bates.

'Germans, Russians, British, what's the difference? They're enemy, captain.'

A flash of lightning filled Millington's empty office. The Doctor and Ace hurried inside.

'There it is!' Ace reached for the chess set on the table, with the parish record book lying next to it.

'No, don't!'

But it was too late. Ace had moved the chess board. There was a slight click as she did so, and a fine wire fell from the board. The safety pin of a grenade was fastened to the other end of the wire.

A chemical grenade rolled across the table and fell

off the edge. The Doctor dived to catch it, but missed
by a fraction of a second. Gas was already starting to
trickle out of the grenade. Without even stopping to
think, the Doctor scooped up a metal waste paper bin
and dropped it over the grenade, sealing off the toxic
gas.

The Doctor and Ace looked at each other. Ace
sighed.

'Thanks. But I don't know why he used a chemical
grenade. I'd have nailed a few stick of explosive under
the table.'

The Doctor twisted round to look under the table.
To his horror, he saw four stick of explosive and a
timing device. The timer read eight seconds remaining. 'Run!' he cried.

They threw themselves out of the door and away
from the hut, racing to get as far away as possible.
The enormous explosion blew them to the ground,
and bricks and debris hurled through the air. The
Doctor and Ace rolled through the mud, and finally
lay still in the pouring rain.

Ace turned to the Doctor. 'I don't understand . . .
A timing device – why? If he'd used direct detonation,
he'd have blown us apart.'

'It's not Millington, it's Fenric. Nothing is what it
seems. Everything is a trap. He's playing with us.'

The Doctor looked at the piece of debris lying
beside him in the mud. It was all that was left of the
parish records. A few burnt pages, the ink smeared
with mud and rain.

'What was in the book?' asked Ace.

'Names.'

'Whose names?'

'Local families. Very old local families. Like Wainwright, Judson, Millington, Dudman . . .'

Suddenly Ace looked up. 'Dudman! Kathleen – she's got a chess set!'

'No, Millington had all the chess sets burnt.'

'Not Kathleen's! I saw it in her suitcase!'

The Doctor scrambled to his feet. 'Come on, before Fenric finds out!'

Sorin and Vershinin lay crouched in the mud along-side the dead bodies of naval guards. Their skin was blistered from the chemical mist. As Sorin looked around, he saw other bodies, some of the British, others Russian. It was impossible to tell them apart.

'We're the last two, the only ones left of Operation Sea-Wolf.'

Vershinin was sick to his stomach. 'This isn't war: it's massacre!'

'Massacre is war. The Ultima machine has done it.'

Vershinin turned to him. 'Destroy it!'

3

The remaining marines were grouped round the old pit building that housed the laboratory. There was no gunfire, only the storm.

Leigh looked round the muddy camp. 'Are they all dead?'

Bates tried to make out any signs of movement amid the wind and rain.

'What's that?' demanded Leigh, as a high-pitched screeching broke out behind them.

'Look out!' cried a marine.

Leight swung round to face the entrance behind them.

The grotesque shape of a haemovore reached out of the shadows. As it lurched forward, others appeared behind it.

Leigh opened fire, and the creatures momentarily staggered back. But the bullets didn't stop them, and they resumed their advance. Leigh opened fire again, joined by other marines. The bullets ripped open the creatures' flesh; the screeching increased, but still it didn't stop them.

'Pull back!' shouted Bates. 'Everybody get out of here!'

But it was too late for some of the marines, whose lives were draining from their veins.

The monstrous figure of Ingiger faced Fenric in the laboratory.

Fenric's eyes burned red. 'At last, another of the wolves of Fenric is summoned to play his role.'

The ancient Ingiger spoke. The voice was part-woman's, and it seemed to fade away in echoes. 'My world is dead.'

'Hardly a great loss if you're the best that evolution could manage. So this is what the human race will come to?'

'Dead.'

'That is in the future. This planet doesn't become your world for thousands of years. First you must engineer the catastrophe that wipes out *Homo sapiens*. Force the genetic remnants to mutate to survive!'

Millington rushed in. 'Your creatures are killing my men!'

He stopped dead when he saw the ghastly figure of Ingiger. 'What is it?'

Fenric turned to him. 'I suppose you could call it the Great Serpent.'

'And the Great Serpent shall rise from the sea and spew venom over all the Earth.'

Fenric's gaze spanned the rows and rows of chemical weapons. 'There's enough poison here to contaminate the Earth for ever!'

Bates, hidden in the shadows of the doorway, listened in horror. This was insane evil! It had to be destroyed!

Silently, he crept outside and ran out into the crashing storm. He must radio for help.

The rain whipped against his face as he slipped and ran through the mud towards the radio hut. The door was banging wildly in the wind. He ran inside and looked at the damaged radio equipment, searching for something that could be made to work. Even a Morse key would do – anything to get a message to the outside world.

There was a movement behind him.

He spun round with his pistol.

Standing in the doorway were the Doctor and Ace. The Doctor looked at Bates. 'The radio equipment's useless. Your radio operator tried it – before the creatures found him.' The Doctor indicated a body lying on the floor.

Bates lowered his gun. 'They're insane! They're going to destroy the world with chemical weapons!'

'All part of Fenric's games.' The Doctor stepped into the room, followed by Ace. Sorin appeared in the doorway behind them.

Bates quickly raised his pistol to the Russian. Sorin didn't move.

Slowly, Bates returned his gun to its holster. 'I agree. We join forces against the real enemy.'

The Doctor wasted no time. 'We've got to find Kathleen's chess set. Ace, you come with me. You two, just give me as much time as you can. Come on, Ace!'

Ace turned quickly to look at Sorin.

Sorin saw the look, and smiled. 'Take care, *tavarisch*.'

The creatures were everywhere in the camp. They hid in the shadows and waited to drop from above or burst from below.

Leigh kicked open the door of the signal monitoring room and threw himself inside. He was followed by two other marines. They swung round with their guns, but there were no creatures inside, only half-a-dozen Wrens who cowered in the corner.

'It's all right, girls!' barked Leigh. 'We'll take care of everything now! You two, the windows!'

The two marines dropped down behind the windows and smashed some panes of glass to get a clear line of fire. Leigh pushed a huge table against the door, sealing it shut, and then crouched down with the other two. They scanned the storm outside, looking for haemovores.

Behind them, the Wrens smiled. They had ghastly white faces and bloated red lips. They stepped from the shadows towards the three marines. A screeching filled the room and the marines turned around just in time to see the creatures' glittering nails slash through the air.

Kathleen held Audrey tight, rocking her gently and trying to protect her from the storm and the fear outside. A flash of lightning filled the Wrens' quarters.

Kathleen froze as she heard a sound from outside the door. The door swung open.

The Doctor and Ace rushed in, and Kathleen cried out in relief.

Ace ran to Kathleen and put her arms round both Kathleen and the baby. 'It's all right, I'll look after you.'

'Ace,' called the Doctor, 'chess set.'

'In the suitcase,' shouted Ace.

The Doctor threw open the suitcase and grabbed the chess board and box of pieces. 'Come on!'

'Don't go!' cried Kathleen. 'Please, don't leave us.'

Ace turned on the Doctor. 'I'll stay here. We can't leave them alone.'

'Don't leave the hut,' ordered the Doctor. He ran out of the door.

Ace ran to the door and closed it. She looked around. 'We've got to do something about those windows. Make sure the creatures can't get through.'

'Under the mattresses!'

Ace grabbed a mattress on one of the bunks and hauled it off. Underneath, the bed was made of loose wooden planks. Ace started collecting them up.

'And there's a tool-kit in the cleaning cupboard!'

In the flash of lightning as it illuminated Dr Judson's office, tears were streaming down Nurse Crane's face. She backed away in terror, as two haemovores emerged from the shadows.

'Nurse Crane.' Dr Judson's voice came from the darkness behind the two creatures. Nurse Crane froze. Dr Judson stepped forward, but now Fenric controlled his body. Nurse Crane stared at him.

Fenric smiled. 'You've looked after this body all these years. Almost like a mother. Watching over

169

everything Dr Judson did. Treating him like a child. And reporting everything you saw to your controllers in Moscow.'

The creatures closed in on the terrified woman.

Fenric's eyes glowed with hatred. 'I feel this is the death Dr Judson would have wished for you.'

The Doctor was alone in the laboratory. He swept a pile of notebooks to the floor to make space on a bench.

Quickly he laid out the chess board and took a handful of pieces. He stared at the board, trying to remember – trying to remember the positions from a game played almost two thousand years ago.

'Where do the pawns go? It's so long ago . . .'

Ace had nailed boards over all the windows, and the only light now came from a small oil lamp that Kathleen had lit. Ace went to sit beside Kathleen, who was rocking Audrey. Tears were running down Kathleen's face. 'What kind of a world is this to grow up in?' she wept.

Ace put her arms round Kathleen. 'They'll have to kill me before I'll let them harm Audrey.' She hugged Kathleen close.

The contents of Kathleen's suitcase were scattered on the floor where the Doctor had dropped them. Ace noticed a photograph. Not the picture of Kathleen's husband – a different photo. Ace picked it up and looked at the picture of Audrey.

'Kathleen, this picture?'

Kathleen looked up and smiled. 'Keep it.'

Ace hugged her. 'Thanks.'

Suddenly the boards over the nearest window splintered. An arm burst through and reached for the baby. Kathleen jumped back.

More hands appeared. Ace looked round wildly. Haemovores were banging at the door. There was no way out!

She looked down. 'The floor!'

She grabbed a large screwdriver from the toolbox and rammed it down between two floorboards. With a huge twist, she levered the floorboard up and ripped it away. She grabbed hold of the next one and wrenched it up. Underneath were the foundations of the hut. 'Come on! It's the only way!'

The haemovores were heaving at the door as Kathleen jumped down with the baby and wriggled her way underneath. Ace followed her.

The foundations were dark and muddy, and Audrey cried as they squirmed their way under the hut and away from the creatures. Ace looked round and saw a gap at the far end. 'Over there!'

They struggled towards the gap, and then wriggled out from under the hut. There were no creatures on this side of the hut. Ace helped Kathleen out. 'Look!' she cried, pointing at a Land Rover standing in the mud. 'Come on!'

They ran slipping through the mud. Ace reached the vehicle and grabbed the door, pulling it open. 'Get away from here! Get as far away as you can! Go to London!'

'I can't! I've nowhere to go!'

Ace thought frantically. Who did she know living in London in 1943? 'Find Streatham! My nan'll look after you! 17 Old Terrace, Streatham – got that? Say it!'

'17 Old Terrace.'

Ace took one last look at Audrey, who was crying in the storm. 'I'll always love you,' she said softly, and leaned forward to kiss the baby.

A screeching sound began to fill the air, and Ace saw two haemovores coming towards them.

'Get going!'

Kathleen jumped into the Land Rover and laid Audrey on a pile of sacks in the back. Then she started the engine and rammed it into gear. The engine screamed and the Land Rover leaned forward, but it didn't move. The wheels spun uselessly in the mud.

'Sacks!' shouted Ace. 'We need a couple of those sacks!'

Kathleen jumped out and threw a sack to Ace. Ace dropped down into the mud and shoved the sack under the wheel, while Kathleen ran round to the other side with the second sack.

The pure fluid of life . . .

The words filled Ace's mind. She shook her head, trying to clear her thoughts, and saw haemovores all around them.

'Quick!' she screamed at Kathleen.

There was nowhere else for either of them to go, so Ace jumped into the Land Rover as well. Kathleen was beside her now, in the passenger seat. Ace slammed the gears into first and slowly let the clutch out. Hands clawed at the windows, and a creature slithered onto the Land Rover's bonnet. Slowly, the vehicle inched forward as the wheels bit into the sacks. Ace let out the clutch more and pushed her foot down on the accelerator. The Land Rover lurched forward. Ace pushed down further on the accelerator and the vehicle began to pick up speed. The haemovores at the sides were left behind, but there was still a creature right in front of them on the bonnet, its sucker trying to break through the windscreen.

Ace pressed her foot right down and accelerated straight at the creatures in front of the vehicle. There were a number of thumps as she drove right through them. They were clear of the other creatures now, but still the one clung on to the windscreen and bonnet. Ace twisted the wheel one way and then twisted it the other. The creature rolled about on the bonnet. Then Ace stood on the brakes.

Its grip weakened by all the twisting, the creature bounced off the bonnet and fell to the ground. Ace threw the wheel round, and spun the Land Rover round the creature in the mud.

Then she braked and threw open the driver's door. 'Remember, 17 Old Terrace. Nan'll look after you!'

She jumped out, and Kathleen slid across into the driver's seat. Ace slammed the door. 'Now go!'

Kathleen put her foot down, and the Land Rover raced away. Ace watched as it headed towards the main gates. The gates were closed, but the Land Rover didn't slow down. Lightning flashed as it hurtled forward, and smashed straight through the gates. Thunder crashed, but the Land Rover was racing away into the distance now. Nothing could catch it!

Ace turned back to the haemovores. Jean and Phyllis stood among them. Ace looked down at the photograph in her hands. At least the creatures wouldn't get the baby.

The haemovores began to close in on her.

The Doctor hesitated for a moment, then placed the final chess-piece on the board. Two kings and a few pawns, in end-game position.

'There.'

A flash of lightning from outside seemed to electrify the board.

* * *

The flash bleached the old pit head white. Fenric gasped slightly.

'The Time Lord has made his move.'

He turned to Ingiger, who held two large flasks of concentrated toxin.

'Take the poisons,' ordered Fenric. 'Carry them through the oceans and release them into the waters.'

'And the haemovores?' The creature's half-woman voice disappeared into androgynous echoes.

'Yes, they've been so useful. How could we have managed without them?' Fenric's face hardened. 'You know how to kill them.'

Ingiger nodded. The veins on its skull began to bulge as it summoned all its psychic power and concentrated on one thought.

Die!

Ace looked in horror as Jean and Phyllis screamed in pain.

Die!

The thought pierced the haemovores' minds like a shaft of burning steel. They clutched their heads in pain and screamed.

Ace tried to cover her ears, but it was a mindscream and it wouldn't stop. The haemovores fell to the ground in agony. Ace saw the two girls twisting in torture, but there was nothing she could do to help them. Their faces began to change. Their skin wrinkled and their bodies grew old. The flesh decomposed and burned from their bones. The other haemovores were the same. Twelve centuries caught up with the creatures in a few seconds.

Finally, the mind-scream stopped. The bodies were still. Nothing remained except smoking skeletons that lay in pools of slime.

* * *

174

Fenric looked round the laboratory. 'Where is the game, Time Lord?'

The Doctor was standing by the chess game. 'Couldn't resist it, could you? The game of traps.'

The Doctor stood aside as Fenric approached the board. He stared at the positions, transfixed. The Doctor looked at him.

'The contest as before, Fenric. One move only. Find the winning move. Spring the trap on me, if you can.'

It was a risk. But at least this gave the Doctor more time. He must find Ingiger.

Vershinin ran into the decryption room and pulled a pair of chain-cutters from his belt. The central rotor unit of the Ultima machine had to be destroyed. He levered the cutters shut and the padlock on the central rotor unit shattered and fell to the floor.

'I'm afraid you've had a wasted journey, Corporal.'

Vershinin spun round. Two shots cracked out and the Russian fell to his knees. He looked up in pain.

Millington emerged from the shadows and stared at him. 'But then, you were never really our allies, were you? Your country will always be the enemy.'

'See you in hell!' spat Vershinin.

'I doubt it.' A final shot cracked out.

Vershinin fell dead to the floor.

Millington looked up. Bates stood in the doorway, his pistol pointing at the commander. Millington stared at him. 'Are you going to use that gun?'

Bates hesitated.

Millington stepped towards him. 'You know your problem, Captain Bates? You don't know who the enemy is. A traitor is someone who doesn't know who the enemy is.'

Millington slowly raised his pistol. Two more shots

175

cracked out, and Bates fell to the ground gasping. Millington strode over him and left him.

Cautiously, Ace went into the laboratory.

'Who's there?' hissed a voice. 'Is that you, Time Lord?'

Ace froze. Fenric was crouched over the chess board as though his body had lost some of its strength. 'Tell me the solution, Time Lord. The contest is too much for this weak human body. Tell me!' He looked up at Ace.

'I don't know the solution.'

'Tell me! You must tell me!'

His head fell back down to stare at the board. Ace backed out in fear.

Ingiger carried the large flasks of toxin down to the cellar beneath the old pit head building, and made for the entrance to the old mine tunnel.

'I've been waiting.' The Doctor stepped out of the shadows.

Ingiger looked at him. 'You know me?' asked the part-woman's voice.

The Doctor nodded. 'Thousands of years in the future, when the Earth is dying – the surface rotting in a chemical slime. Half a million years of industrial progress.'

'I am the last – the last living creature on Earth.' Ingiger's voice was full of sadness. 'I watched my world dying in the acid mists. I saw my children die in the chemicals. I could do nothing.'

'And then, at your moment of pain, you're carried back tens of thousands of years in a time storm to Transylvania. And made to wait a thousand years more.'

'He brought me back in time. Without the flask I was trapped.'

'Ah yes, the flask. I imprisoned him like an evil genie.'

'Only he can return me to the future.'

'So, like a faithful servant, you followed the flask across Europe. Followed the merchant who brought it from Constantinople. Followed the Viking pirates who stole it. Followed it here.'

'My waiting is over. Once I have completed my task, he will return me to my time.'

'Another of Fenric's games. The Butterfly Effect. At a crucial point in the Earth's climatic pattern, a butterfly beats its wing. This tiny disturbance upsets the delicate balance in the atmosphere. The turbulence multiplies, until finally violent storms erupt on the other side of the globe. All from a butterfly's wing.' The Doctor looked at Ingiger. 'Think of those chemicals you're carrying. Which will be the droplet that finally overloads the Earth's fragile balance? Which will be the molecule that kills your children?'

The Mosin-Nagant 7.62mm bolt-action repeating rifle gave a series of loud metallic clicks as Sorin snapped the bolt forward and locked a fresh cartridge into the chamber. The Mosin-Nagant bolt-action repeater was less fashionable than the Tokarev semi-automatic – it was older and much less sophisticated – but it was reliable. And a single bullet was all that Sorin needed now.

'It's time to die, Fenric.'

Fenric looked up. His body was dying, and he barely had the strength to hold himself up. His eyes were no more than a feeble red glow.

'Where have you been?' Fenric's voice was weak.

177

He saw Sorin's rifle pointing at him. 'You still don't understand, do you? Why do you think you were selected for this mission?'

Sorin's voice was steady. 'Because I speak English. My grandmother was English.'

'Yes, Miss Emily Wilson, granddaughter of Joseph Sundvik. You are touched by the curse of Fenric. I selected you! You are one of the wolves of Fenric!'

Sorin squeezed the trigger.

A flash of lightning flooded the decryption room with stark monochrome, and Ace's heart stopped. Lying on the ground she saw the dead body of Vershinin; next to him lay Bates.

She hardly dared think.

A movement caught her eye, and she heard a sound from Bates.

Ace knelt beside him and took his hand. 'What happened?' she asked.

The captain opened his eyes and looked at her. He was close to death, and his voice was barely a whisper. 'War . . . a game played by politicians. We were just pawns in a game.'

Then the faint trace of a smile crossed his lips. 'But the pawns are fighting together now, eh?' he struggled. 'We're fighting tog – '

He didn't finish the word.

Ace felt his hand go limp, and she saw his face was empty.

She put his hand down, and wept.

Now she understood. The winning move in the game.

Time passed, and the rain beat down outside. Finally, Ace left the dead bodies and turned to go. But she was tired and worn down. The deaths had no

178

meaning, no significance. Bates and Vershinin, lying dead where they fell. Jean and Phyllis – only kids, and all they wanted was to be loved for what they were. But there was nothing but emptiness for them.

Ace walked through the rain. Mud-soaked bodies lay everywhere. How many did it take?

The laboratory was quiet. Sorin was standing over the dead body of Fenric. Or was it the dead body of Dr Judson?

What was the difference? It was dead.

The chess-pieces stood unmoved on the board. An end-game without conclusion. Ace looked at Sorin. He stood over Judson's body with his eyes closed, as though waiting.

'Fenric would never have guessed the solution anyway.' Her voice was empty.

'Tell me, *tavarisch*.'

'A simple move. The black and white pawns don't fight each other. They join forces.'

'Thank you – child.'

The sudden realization gripped Ace's heart.

'Ace! Don't!' screamed the Doctor, bursting through the door.

But it was too late. The Russian captain raised his head and opened his eyes. In horror, Ace saw Fenric's evil blazing red in the Russian captain's eyes. Sorin was dead, and Fenric now controlled his body!

Fenric reached out to the chess board. He move one of the white pawns and knocked down the white king with it. 'Black wins, Time Lord!'

A massive bolt of lightning ripped through the heavens, and smashed through the laboratory roof. A blinding livid-white light pierced the air and instantly carbonized the chess figures. White-hot sparks flew out, setting fire to wooden benches and crates.

179

Ace backed away from Fenric. 'What's happened?'

Fenric smiled. 'The wolves of Fenric – descendants of the Viking who first buried the flask. All pawns in my game. Dr Judson, Commander Millington, Captain Sorin, the ancient haemovore and now you.'

'Me? You can't . . . How?'

'The baby. In thirty years, the baby will be grown. She will have a daughter. That daughter will be you. You've just created your own future!'

He took the photograph from Ace, held it up to her gaze and laughed. 'The baby is your mother. The mother you hate!'

Ace turned to escape. But the monstrous Ingiger was standing behind her. She had nowhere to go!

The burning laboratory began to crackle all around her.

'Judson!'

Millington's cry rang out. The commander ran forward and fell down beside Judson's body.

Fenric laughed, and then looked at Ingiger. 'Kill them all,' he ordered. 'Kill them slowly.'

Something burned inside Ace. A deep anger that flamed up. 'You don't stand a chance! Tell him, Doctor. Tell him he's got it wrong.'

The Doctor didn't move.

Fenric's expression was victorious. 'The Time Lord has failed. The wolves of Fenric have released me.'

'He never fails.' Ace's voice was defiant and strong. 'If I believe in anything, I believe in the Doctor. Complete faith.'

A golden swell of sound burst in the air – the majestic chorus voiced by Ace's pure faith in the Doctor. Ingiger reeled backwards, and clutched his head in pain, as the psychic carillon rang through his mind.

180

'Clever,' observed Fenric. 'The creature can't penetrate her psychic force field.'

He turned to the Doctor. 'Time for one final game, then.'

He put on a black rubber glove and picked a small ampoule from the bench. It glowed green with the deadly toxin. Fenric held it out towards Ace. 'The choice is yours, Time Lord. I shall kill you anyway – but if you want the girl to live, kneel down before me.'

The Doctor still didn't move.

'I believe in you!' cried Ace.

Fenric grew impatient. 'Kneel,' he snapped, 'if you want the girl to live.'

The Doctor's face didn't change.

'Kill her,' he said.

Fenric smiled, and his smile grew into a laugh. 'The Time Lord finally understands!'

The Doctor's eyes were dark. 'You think I didn't know? A baby with the same name as her mother? I knew.'

'Longer ago than that, Time Lord. Ever since Iceworld, where you first met the girl.'

'I knew right from the start. You think I'd have chosen a social misfit like her, if I hadn't known? She couldn't even pass the chemistry exams at school, yet somehow she managed to create a time storm in her bedroom? I saw your hand in it from the very beginning.'

What was he saying? Ace stared in disbelief. She trusted him completely, and now he was betraying her. 'Professor . . . No . . .'

The Doctor didn't even look at her. 'She's an emotional cripple. I wouldn't waste my time on her unless I could use her somehow.'

The words twisted in Ace like a knife. 'No!'

She fell to her knees; the glorious sound vanished. The laboratory was in flames all around, crackling fiercely.

Fenric turned to Ingiger. 'Kill them now!'

Ingiger moved towards Fenric. Its lonely voice filled the burning building. 'My world is dead! You must die too!'

'No, I command you!'

But Ingiger forced Fenric back, backwards into the flames.

'Come on!' cried the Doctor to Ace.

Ace was sobbing on the floor. 'Leave me alone!'

'We've got to get out!' The Doctor grabbed Ace's arm.

'Leave me alone!' she screamed.

But the Doctor dragged her to her feet, and pulled her towards the door.

'Millington!' he called back. 'Millington, get out!'

Millington turned to look at the Doctor. His face was sad with grief. He shook his head, and turned back to Judson's dead body. He picked the body up, and held it in his arms in a distorted pietà.

The flames were everywhere. 'You must, Millington!' called the Doctor, trying to fight his way back through the fires. A huge burning roof beam splintered above him, and crashed down, cutting him off from the commander. The Doctor tried to see through the scorching fires, but Millington was lost.

The Doctor turned and grabbed Ace again, dragging her through the burning doorway. Once outside, he didn't stop, but dragged her slipping through the mud until they heard a huge crash from behind them. They fell to their knees, and saw the roof and walls of the blazing building collapse inwards in a fireburst shower of sparks. Everyone inside was dead.

Ace knelt sobbing in the mud. 'I couldn't even pass the chemistry exams.'

The Doctor tried to explain. 'I'm sorry, Ace. I'd have done anything rather than hurt you. But it was the only way. Your faith in me was holding the ancient haemovore back, and I knew it was on our side.'

'You said I was a social misfit, an emotional cripple.'

'It had to be something that would break your faith in me.'

'Full marks for teenage psychology!'

'Look at me, Ace. Ever since I've known you, I've known you were part of the trap. I've known, and I didn't tell you. I let Fenric manipulate you, because I knew that way you would lead me to him. I suppose I've been manipulating you too. And now you've discovered it, you think I've betrayed you. You hate me, just like you say you hate your mum and dad.'

'What's wrong with me? She's my mum, and I don't love her. What's wrong with me?'

'You loved the baby.'

'But I didn't know she was my mum.'

'Think about it. Do you really hate her or is it a confused tangle of feelings – love, hate, joy and grief – all mixed up? You can love someone and hate them at the same time.'

The sky was clear over Maidens' Point. Ace stood on a ledge in the cliff-side, staring down into the deep waters. The undercurrents churned beneath, spinning eddies on the surface. A silent tear ran down her face.

'Love and hate are frightening feelings,' said the Doctor, 'especially when one of them is trapped struggling beneath the surface.'

Ace wiped her face. She looked down into the dark

183

waters. She took a step forward and jumped, diving down towards the sea. Her body seemed to hang in the air as she plummeted down. Then she hit the surface and sliced into the water.

The vortex of undercurrents engulfed her and dragged her down, deep down. She struggled to escape, kicking uselessly agains the powerful forces. Figures spiralled in the torrents, and as they whirled around her, Ace saw their faces. This one hate – a figure in chains, forever possessed by the overwhelming need to destroy, to annihilate utterly. It had an adult body, but the expression was that of a furious, red-faced baby, screaming its hatred at the universe. This one grief – the face seeming to cry out in one long, heart-broken wail. Sobbing for the past that was lost forever. This one love – its arms reaching to embrace, and its eyes full of deep, boundless understanding. This one want – an expression that ached with hunger and need. This one joy – eyes of indissoluble delight. Bright with a pleasure that knew no bounds. This one sex – laughter, lechery and animal passion. A whorehouse of enjoyment.

As the dozens of figures whirled past in a dizzying waltz, Ace finally realised that they all had her face. Her face full of hate; her face full of love; her face full of guilt; her face full of joy. They were all her. Every emotional strand of her feelings, set free and dancing single. Grief, fury, joy, hate, fear, want, love, wonder. They were all part of her. Some good, some bad, some hidden away for years so she'd forgotten they were there.

She reached out to touch them, and know them all again. The rush of emotions that filled every part of her. The thrill of feelings that made her alive! Twisting round and round as the spiral vortex carried her down, faster and faster, tumbling through torrents, cascades of turmoil, until finally she was free again – drifting calmly through the deep blue waters. The vortex had gone, the figures disappeared, and the feelings were inside her once more, restored to their natural balance. Love, hate, joy, fear – they were all hers again. Natural feelings she had forced down into the undercurrents of her spirit, but they were free at last. And for the first time since she was a small child, she felt whole.

She swam easily through the clear blue waters. Above her, the surface sparkled in the sunlight. She kicked upwards, and the waters grew lighter and lighter, until finally she burst through into the bright sunny day. The waves splashed around her, and she gasped in the fresh warm breeze.

The woman threw back her head and laughed. She felt good to be alive!

Epilogue

Dawn

PARIS, 1887. The sun had risen less than an hour earlier, but already it smiled down over the Jardin des Tuileries. A young lady and an older gentleman strolled through the gardens and enjoyed the fresh morning sunshine. A light breeze rustled through the trees where birds were singing, and a squirrel scampered in front of the two walkers and disappeared up among the branches. Beyond the gardens, the river flowed gracefully under the bridges and the first of the day's carriages clattered over the cobbles. Secluded among the trees and fountains, however, the two walkers strolled in peace.

Finally the young woman spoke.

'You were wrong, weren't you?' she said, smiling at the older gentleman from beneath her parasol.

'When?' he asked.

'Years ago, you told me about good and evil.'

'I told you many things.'

'But you told me about good and evil, two forces from the dawn of time. Two forces, you said.'

'Ah,' a slight smile appeared on his face, 'perhaps that was a bit of an oversimplification.'

The young lady's laugh sparkled like silver.

'You were younger then, Dorothée,' explained the gentleman. 'Young minds like to understand the world in terms of opposites. Good and evil, love and hate, heaven and hell, friend and enemy . . .'

'But you showed me that love and hate are not opposites.'

'Did I? I forget.'

'You know you did!' Another silvery laugh.

The gentleman sighed. 'If only everyone could see the world like you do — realize that good and evil don't exist . . . have never existed. Only nature exists. And nature is always beautiful, whether it's a fiery erupting volcano, or . . . or . . .' He struggled for another example.

'Or these delightful gardens?' offered the young lady.

The gentleman laughed. 'Just so, my dear!'

He looked around and admired the beauty of the lawns and statues, and the magnificence of the trees beyond. 'You know, I told Louis that this would be a good place for a garden. He wanted to build the palace here, but I said, "You take my advice, Louis — build the palace over there and put the gardens by the river."'

'You're changing the subject.'

'Ah.'

'If only nature exists, then who, or what, was Fenric?'

'A part of nature, of course, just like you and I.'

'An evil part?'

'No, simply a part that was out of balance. Nature is a perfect balance — a harmony between good and evil, between love and hate, between heaven and hell. Evil can exist only in harmony with good.'

187

'Just like love only exists with hate. Sunrise and sunset.'

'If only people could see the balance in nature, I'm— sure they'd be a lot happier.'

A pocket watch chimed softly. The gentleman pulled it from his waistcoat. 'Good heavens, 1887. I really should be going.'

'Oh, no, stay until this evening, please.' The young lady tugged at his arm. 'I haven't seen you for years, and I was hoping you'd come to the ball. There's someone I want you to meet.'

The older gentleman looked at the young lady.

She blushed and smiled. 'You won't be cross, will you? He's a young count from St Petersburg – Count Sorin. He's the perfect image of his great-grandson! And I think I've fallen hopelessly in love with him.'

The older gentleman frowned. 'There are times when I wonder what I've done to your species' gene pool. If your children's ears stick out, don't blame me,' he grumbled.

The young lady laughed and took his arm. Together they walked off towards the Pont Royal.

And what happened after that, we shall never know, because every story must have a beginning, middle, and

[END]